Her Place in
TIME

BETTY JOSEY PARBS

Book Vine Press
2516 Highland Dr.
Palatine, IL 60067

Chapter 1

Annie looked around wondering where she was, everything was so strange and eerie, this is a part of Boston I have never seen she thought to herself. Everything was so quiet, not even the sound of a horn from an impatient driver, none of the usual traffic noise. The silence was broken by a deep rumbling growing louder and sounding closer. Turning, she saw a faint outline of a horse and its rider. As it got nearer to her, she could see the figure atop the large creature. She stood frozen, confused thoughts running through her mind, then she turned and began running. The grass was wet beneath her bare feet and the loose stones felt like needles going deep into her skin. The full moon illuminated the strange countryside that lay before her but it did not help, she was lost. The faster Annie ran the louder the galloping became until it became a pounding in her ears.

All of a sudden, Annie felt herself falling into darkness unlike anything she had ever seen before. Then something…or someone grabbed her wrist.

"Hang on lass, I got you."

Annie awoke with a jolt instead of slowly and reluctantly, she looked around her small cheerful bedroom as if to reassure herself of her existence. Yes, she was surrounded by her most precious possessions, including the doll her father had given her for her third birthday. It was the doll that didn't say "Ma-Ma" anymore. There on the bookshelf were the shells from the beach that she had so tenderly scooped up in her arms when she was five. On the wall was the first place ribbon she had won at twelve, for running faster than Mary Jo, her bitter rival in the seventh grade. Her gaze paused when she saw the wedding picture of her parents; it had always made her smile and feel less afraid. The smiling faces gave her a feeling of love and comfort. There had always been such happiness when they were alive. She silently cursed the drunk driver that had taken them away. Annie had come to terms with the tragedy but still had misgivings at times of stress.

But why was her heart still pounding so? She did not remember the dream that she had had, if, in fact, she had dreamt at all. Annie waited for her heart to slow down and then she got out of bed but when her feet touched the floor she felt a stinging, must be the new shoes she thought.

She went to the kitchen area of her one bedroom apartment, reached up into the cupboard and retrieved the small canister of gourmet coffee. It was one of the few luxuries she allowed herself. After measuring the grounds and starting her two-cup coffee maker, she walked slowly to the bathroom and began filling her tub, as she did every morning. She returned to the kitchen, poured a cup of coffee. Annie sipped the hot coffee while waiting for the tub to fill rinsed the cup and returned to the bathroom.

She lay in the warm water she thought about her family heritage. She had been doing her family tree recently and found that her ancestors who came from Scotland & England had then married into the Cherokee Indian lineage. In fact, on her mother's side, her great-great grandmother had been a full Cherokee and her grandmother, again on her mother's side, was half Cherokee too. After much additional research and the kind help of Mrs. Helfriche at the public library, she had even found out both of their names. Her great-grandmother's name was Narsissa and her grandmother was named Arkansas. It was so interesting…she really loved her heritage and was very proud to be of Cherokee linage…now she would be checking into the Scottish and English parts of herself… It was all so fascinating.

She reached out for the bar of soap; she noticed the bruise on her wrist. It had not been there yesterday and, try as she might, Annie could not remember hitting anything. Even more puzzling was the shape of the mark. It resembled a handprint. She put her wrist up to her nose, not knowing why, and smelled a strange scent. It seemed to be that of leather.

"Leather?" she thought. "I haven't been around any leather lately."

Quickly she examined her other wrist, and felt relieved when it was found to be unmarked, only her right wrist had the strange impression.

She slid down in the bathtub and tipped her head back to wash her hair. As she reached up to lather her hair, her hand touched something. She jerked upright, and saw bits of grass falling into the water.

"What in the world! I have what looks like grass falling out of my hair she said aloud. Annie went on and washed her hair then started to shave her leg; she saw little nicks and bruising on her feet. This is too damn weird she thought; I must be walking in my sleep, she had heard stress could cause things like that.

Annie looked at the clock on the bathroom counter, "My God!" It was 6:25 and she had to be at work by 7:00. She would have to sort all this out late when she had more time. After quickly drying herself and after fluffing her short hair she threw on her scrubs and flew out the door.

Annie's apartment was only two blocks from Boston General Hospital, so she made it to work with time to spare. As she ran up the stairs she smiled at all the cheerfully colored cartoons painted on the walls. It helped to put the children as ease and made their stay a little easier. Annie was happy she had chosen to work on the children's floor she loved kids and hoped to have several someday.

At the morning briefing, Annie found out that Joey, a ten-year-old boy that she'd been taking care of, off and on, had been readmitted during the night. Joey was diagnosed with bone cancer six months ago and things did not look too bright for him. She has been his primary nurse from the moment he was admitted to the unit, fortunately, she was assigned to him again today.

Joey was small for his age but was such a handsome boy, with sandy hair that never stayed in place. Laughter seemed to bubble up in his little body until he could no longer contain it and the nurses delighted in caring for him. Joey took everything in stride, never complaining, even about being home schooled Annie knew he enjoyed going to school when possible and that he missed all of his friends. The hospital did not allow many visitors, in order to keep Joey as germ free as possible, so his family visited as much as they possibly could.

Joey had a younger sister, Suzie, who had just started the first grade. He often told Annie how much of a pain in the neck she was. "Girls!" he would say, rolling his eyes, "Why do we need them?" Annie would just laugh and tell him to wait a few years, things would change and then he would know. Joey would narrow his eyes and simply say, "I'll never like girls." Annie knew that he really did love and miss his little sister. He kept a picture of her in a Winnie the Pooh frame on his night table, alongside the one of his parents in its ornate silver frame.

Joey's parents were at the hospital every day taking care of all his every wants and needs. Annie had talked with them on numerous occasions and found them to always be as positive as possible with Joey. They were always very honest with him and encouraged Annie and the other staff to do the same. They never wanted to lie to their son. Joey secretly respected and loved them very much for being that way.

Little Suzie was a real cutie. Aside from the picture on Joey's night table, Annie had permitted Joey's parents to smuggle her in to see Joey a couple of times. She had been so thrilled that she had hugged Annie's neck and said, "Thanks miss Annie." She was a tiny little lady in her ruffled dresses and Mary Jane shoes. Her white-blond ringlets haloed her head and when she smiled it lit up her face. What a little cherub!!

As Annie entered Joey's room, she was hit smack in the chest by a nerf-basketball. "Oh!" shouted Joey. "I'm sorry. I was trying for another basket."

Annie just laughed and tossed the ball back. "Well, I see we are off to a fine start," she replied with a warm smile. "I just wanted to look in on you, I will see you later."

Annie's day was progressing slowly but she knew things could get wild after a while. She only had several minor emergencies and six children were released. The little girl in the room next to Joey's pulled her I.V. tubing out of her arm, Annie laughingly scolded her, reinserted the tube, and things went along smoothly after that. Lunch was a hurried sandwich, a small carton of milk and some small talk with the young intern who was in her second year. After lunch, Annie worked on her charts and then visited with Joey for awhile, then sat down to finish her charts. About halfway through a code blue was called and off Annie went down the hall.

Her shift finally ended and she walked home, thinking of the children she wanted someday. Happy kids whose noise and affectionate play would bring joy into her dull, lonely life.

After stopping at the neighborhood market to pick up a few things, she went back to her apartment. She could hear her phone ringing as she was struggling with the bags and trying to unlock the door. Before she could set the bags down on the counter the ringing had stopped.

She went to the machine and played back the message. It was from Rita…begging off from their planned dinner. Something had come up. Oh well…just as well…Annie really didn't feel like talking anyway. She made a small supper and after the dishes were finished, curled up on the bed with a good book. She did not read very long before she had fallen fast asleep.

Annie heard the unmistakable sound of a galloping horse. Terrified, she began to run. The full moon illuminated the strange countryside that lay before her. The faster Annie ran the louder the galloping became. Her breath was coming in gasps. She had never been so frightened in her life. Run! Run! She told herself but her feet felt like lead.

Suddenly, Annie felt herself falling into darkness unlike anything she had ever seen before. Then something…or someone grabbed her wrist.

"Hang on lass, I got you."

She looked up into the most beautiful eyes she had ever seen. They belonged to a face she didn't know, but she instinctively knew she could trust. His broad shoulders made him look like a football player. The most unsettling thing was that she seemed to have been here once before. The scent of leather and the smell of a sweaty horse filled her nostrils as he lowered her safely to solid ground.

The man sternly asked in a strong brogue, "Why are you out on the moors at such an ungodly hour and all by your self Lassie?"

Annie could not speak. She did not know what he was talking about. Moors? What did he mean? She wondered. She was cold and shivering, and could not utter a sound. She had never been so bewildered in her life.

The stranger said, "Perhaps some tea will stop your shiverin."

As he shifted his weight and turned his mount, Annie saw that he was atop the biggest, blackest horse she could have ever imagined. Annie was a city girl and was quite frightened by this huge animal. Surely this man did not expect her to ride on this thing she would sooner walk.

Before she had time to react, the man reached down, grasped her wrist and effortlessly swung her up behind him.

"Hold on!" he warned her.

Annie had never traveled so fast on anything that did not have four wheels and an engine. Her fears quickly began to vanish, for this man and horse moved as one. Each seemed to know what the other was thinking. The countryside flew by. They must be deep in a forest for all she could see were trees with hills in the distance. Just as Annie felt she could relax, up ahead there appeared to be a rather wide ditch.

"Did this man intend to have his horse jump over it? Could the horse make such a jump?" she wondered, with renewed fear.

Annie was awakened abruptly by the sound of a horn penetrating the walls of her apartment. She looked at her alarm clock and realized that she had slept all night. She was surprised that it was already 6 a.m. As she put her feet on the floor and stood up, she realized that her legs felt weak.

"Perhaps I should pay better attention to my diet," Annie thought to herself. "And maybe get some regular exercise. After all that sleep, I shouldn't feel this tired."

She made her morning coffee, and went through her ritual as usual. When she was putting on her pantyhose, she noticed the black and blue mark on her inner thigh. Something in her mind made her jump. Something about a very large horse came into her mind.

"That's ridiculous." She thought, "I don't know anything about horses." Annie finished dressing and went to work. But the thought just would not go away.

After report, Annie headed for Joey's room. His parents were visiting, so Annie just looked in, said hello and told them she would return later. Morning rounds passed quickly and before she knew it, it was one o'clock and she was starving. She ate lunch with her best friend, Rita, in the hospital cafeteria. She had known Rita for a little over four years. They had gone through nursing school together and had always attempted to help each other as much as they could. Then, with a stroke of luck, they had wound up together here at Boston General.

"You look awfully tired, Annie. Have you been getting enough sleep? Or have you and Bill been out on late dates?" Rita asked.

"Bill?" laughed Annie.

Bill was a slight, nervous man that Annie had dated, off and on, for a few months. Annie could never be serious about Bill. His mother was the only woman in his life and Annie did not want a momma's boy. Bill was a skilled veterinarian and devoted too much time to his practice. She felt as if he were more comfortable around the animals than he was around people. And yet, there was something she liked about the man. Perhaps it was his compassion for the helpless animals that touched Annie's heart.

"Bill?" she said again, "Rita, you know I've known Bill about eight months now." Rita said, "Yes?"

"And have you ever heard me talk about him in all that time? I mean, really talk about him?" Annie continued.

"Well, no, I guess I haven't." said Rita, "I thought you were just being very private." "Bill is a good man but he is about as exciting as going to the dentist." said Annie with a sigh. He was a very nice looking man, if it had not been for those awful glasses. With all the money he made, Annie couldn't understand why he didn't get some of the new, thinner lenses, or even contact lenses. He hoarded his money, investing in the stock market and never bought things for himself. He pampered his mother, and would, occasionally, take Annie out somewhere fancy to eat. Other than the stocks and his mother he only shelled out money for his practice.

His father had left him and his mother when he was twelve years old and as a result he clung to his mother. Bill had told Annie that someone had to care for her, so he did. His mother had not left the house since her husband had disappeared. Bill did all the shopping and everything that his Mother used to do. He was a good son, but as long as his mother was alive, Bill would never marry.

"Well, what is it then? You look…well…tired is all I can think of. Are they over working you in Pediatrics, or what?" Rita asked.

Annie considered telling Rita about her dreams, but decided against it, after all it was just a silly dream. "No, I'm not being overworked at all I probably just need to read less at night and get more sleep." Annie and Rita went shopping after work, and then enjoyed a pleasant dinner at Annie's apartment talking late into the night.

Rita grew up in the seedy part of Boston and had spent most of her childhood dodging her father's ever present and menacing belt. She did not like to talk about her life before becoming a nurse, but she had confided in Annie. Rita's father was now in prison for manslaughter, after killing a man in a barroom brawl. Her mother had spent the last years of her life in a mental hospital before dying of brain cancer.

In college, Rita was a little older then her classmates, graduating at the age of twenty- four She had been forced to drop out and restart her schooling several times so she could take care of her mother. She worked extra hard and graduated with grades well above average.

Her wish was to someday become a Doctor but that would take more student loans and Rita had enough money problems. Rita was also quiet the party girl and she really loved the men so that was a good excuse. The characteristic Annie loved most about Rita was her big heart. She would do anything she could for anyone if it were within her power. Rita was presently dating Ted a young intern and spent the whole evening going on about him. Rita and Annie finally called it a night at about 10 p.m.

When Annie was alone again, she put the things she had purchased away, placed her soiled uniform in the clothes hamper and got out a fresh one for the next day. Then she washed up, put on her pajamas and went to bed wondering if she might have a dream as strange as her previous one.

"Hold on!" the man shouted to Annie.

She thought she would squeeze this man in half but he seemed to like her arms around him. As the huge animal leaped across the wide ditch, Annie held her breath and closed her eyes tightly. The huge horse soared over the ditch and landed as gently as anything that big could, you can relax now lass the stranger said. When Annie opened her eyes she saw a large stone house ahead she had never seen a house like it before. The man reined in his horse, dismounted and reached up for Annie and lowered her to the ground.

The house was very rustic looking; Annie guessed that it would be called Tudor in design. The framing of the windows and the single door were of wood, which had grown weathered over the years. Thick green vines covered much of the stone Annie guessed that the house must have been around for generations.

An old woman came out to greet them she had a very nice, yet worn face and a full head of silver-gray hair that was braided down her back. Annie thought that the woman might have been in her late fifties. She was a small person and Annie could see that she had worked very hard in her lifetime, as was evident by her callused hands and broken fingernails. As tired as she appeared to be, her face lit up when she looked at the stranger. There was such tenderness in the gestures she made towards him, that she could have been his mother.

The woman stopped short, and asked where he had been, who was the young lady, and why was she here? The man walked over to the old woman, put his arm around her and whispered something in her ear. In the light, which came from inside the house, the old woman looked at Annie and gasped. Her face turned ashen and her knees turned to jelly Annie heard the woman mumble a name but could not understand her.

Annie felt a chill go down her spine and at that moment, the old woman's legs buckled and she slipped to the ground. The stranger caught her lifted her up and started toward the house as Annie rushed to help. She loosened the old woman's collar and a pendant appeared Annie froze staring at the familiar pendent. It was the same kind of pendant that had been passed down to Annie by her grandmother and Annie remembered her mother telling her that it was one of a kind. It was hundreds of years old and had been made for one of her ancestors. All Annie could remember was being told the pendent had come from England.

The story was that the owner of the pendant had been raised by nuns and did not know her parents. The nuns had arranged a marriage for the woman when she had reached the age of sixteen and from written accounts; the young woman had received the pendant on her wedding day. Where it had come from had not been recorded anywhere.

The old woman regained her composure and brushed the stranger away. "I'm fine.

Please let me go and I'll be makin' some tea for your guest. I just got a wee bit light headed." The old woman turned and led them into the house.

Annie followed the stranger, a little reluctantly, into his home "What a strange house." Annie thought to herself. The room they entered appeared to be a large kitchen with a huge wooden table in the middle.

There were three men sitting at the table, playing some kind of game with round chips. All of a sudden, one of the men jumped up from his chair and grabbed the man across from him. Annie thought that there would be a fight, but the stranger stepped in and calmed things down. Annie could not help but stare at the men encircling the table they were very dirty and they had on kilts, crudely made shirts, and boots that seemed to have been made out of animal skins. They all looked like they needed a good hot bath.

Then she noticed that they were starring back at her taking her eyes from the men at the table, Annie looked around the room.

There was a dirt floor and a large stone fireplace that covered most of one whole wall. Pots and pans hung by hooks from the ceiling near the fireplace that was so big a grown man could walk into it. The room looked warm and inviting but everything was so rustic and simple never the less Annie felt cozy and safe as she sat down by the fire.

The stranger sat down beside her and stretched his long legs out towards the blazing logs staring into the fire. Annie looked at him more closely; he had jet-black hair and a large faint scar that ran from his forehead down to his mouth. He had a strong, rough face, yet there was a definite softness in his eyes. His hands were large and toughened, but had a gentleness that she had seen when he had touched the old woman's face outside, after she had fainted.

Looking at the man, Annie began to feel things that she had never felt before. There was a stirring in her heart and goose bumps were on her arms. Zing went the strings of my heart. Annie hummed to herself and laughed softly to herself. The stranger turned to Annie and she felt her cheeks flush because she had been starring.

"Oh! Please excuse me!" Annie felt herself blush when she realized that the stranger was watching her. They both turned as the old woman returned to the room with a pot of hot tea and set it on the hearth in front of them and then excused herself. When the woman had gone, the man cleared his throat and said, "My name is Robert McKenna an this is my home. You are welcome to stay as long as you like. Mary is one of my servants an she will show you to a room for the night. We shall talk in the morning after tea. You need to rest, you look very tired. "

Mary came back into the room with a gown for Annie to sleep in. Annie told Robert goodnight and followed Mary up the dark stairs. They first stopped in the dressing room and Mary helped Annie out of her street clothes and into the nightgown. They then walked down the hallway to a bedroom and entered. Mary turned to Annie and said, "Good evening Miss." Then she turned and retreated back the way they had come.

Annie looked around the room cautiously. It was sparsely furnished with just a bed, a table and small nightstand next to the bed. Annie reached out for the light switch but there was none and she realized there were no lamps. The only light came from a small candle flickering on the nightstand. Maybe Robert was restoring this old house and had not gotten around to installing electricity yet. Annie walked to the bedside, blew out the candle, crawled onto the large bed and fell asleep thinking how soft the mattress felt.

Chapter 2

Annie bolted upright in bed, not knowing exactly where she was. There was a storm in progress. The rain noisily pelted the windows, thunder made the walls vibrate and lighting illuminated the room. Thank goodness she was back in her apartment although the house in the dream was nice, she loved her apartment. After breathing a sigh of relief, Annie remembered that there was no rush to get up because she had the day off. She could be a little lazy today if she wanted to. After much stretching, she stepped out of bed and went to the kitchen where she stopped short in front of the mirror. What did she have on? She carefully examined her reflection. She was wearing a drab, off-white nightgown. It had a high collar; long sleeves and the hemline almost touched the floor. She did not own anything like this. Where had it come from? Strange feelings came over her and she shivered. It was just a dream wasn't it? The man was strange but very interesting. Dreams are not real so what the hell was going on here. Was she losing her mind? "I will go see Doctor Weston," thought Annie, "he is a good psychiatrist and maybe he could sort things out. I need to take better care of myself," Annie said out loud.

After breakfast, she cleaned the apartment and then went to the supermarket. She was out of almost everything, so it took quiet a while to shop. On the way home she stopped and picked up a bouquet of flowers. Back at the apartment, she put everything away and then called Bill. They had a dinner date that night and Annie wanted to beg off but she changed her mind when she heard the disappointment in his voice.

A short time later, Bill and Annie went to a little French restaurant for dinner. As Annie sipped a glass of wine, she studied Bill closely.

Without meaning to, she found herself comparing Bill to the strange man in her dreams. She noticed the nervous twitch in Bill's jaw, and the way he could not make a decision on what to order for dinner. She knew that Bill was different in his professional life. She had seen him make life and death decisions in a split second with a sick or injured animal. He was so sure of his life as a veterinarian, but not as a man. She even felt that he would probably need a *how to* book for his wedding night!

Dinner seemed to drag on forever and she was glad when it ended. She enjoyed the dinner and the funny movie that they went to, but not Bill's company. He was so wrapped up in his own world that he did not have room in it for her. Bill dropped Annie off, kissed her lightly on the lips got back in his car and drove off. She watched as his tail lights faded out of sight...then turned with a sigh to go into her apartment. She stopped short as she stepped up to the door thinking she heard a faint meow. As she turned, she felt something soft brush against her ankle. She reached down and picked up the smallest kitten she had ever seen. The poor little thing was too tiny to be without its mother, so Annie took it into her apartment and gave it some warm milk. She smiled as she watched the kitten eagerly lap it up. The kitten looked better after getting some nourishment, so Annie carried it to bed with her. It curled up in the crook of Annie's arm and after much purring fell asleep.

Annie awoke to the sound of galloping horses. She quickly ran to the window and looked out to see Robert talking to a small group of men. They were too far away to hear anything, but from the gestures she knew that something was wrong. The men were dressed in leather and fur and had long knifes in their belts. Some of them were carrying long swords and their hands were covered with leather gloves. Their horses were magnificent creatures, standing proudly, pawing the ground with eager anticipation. Annie thought that the horses looked better cared for than the men upon them.

Robert gestured for the men to wait, ran into the house, changed his clothes, grabbed his weapons, and returned to mount his waiting horse. After mounting, he turned and looked up to see Annie framed in the window. Their eyes met. Robert smiled, spun Max around and they all rode off.

Annie watched as they rode off and wondered what kind of world she was in. She turned and made up the bed "How drab everything is, yet it is all so fresh and clean," she thought.

She went downstairs to inquire about Robert's departure and found a man sitting by the fire. As she entered the kitchen the huge man attempted to rise but sat back down with a grimace of pain.

"Mornin Miss." Mary said. "this is Hagis MacGregor, one of Robert's men. He is going to be here for awhile because he got kicked by his horse."

"Oh my goodness!" Annie said "Where are you hurt?"

"Oh he will be fine." Mary said "He is too mean to be hurt bad."

"I just messed up my ribs a little." the man said. "I will be fine after Mary fixes me." Mary had a wide piece of cloth and started to wrap it around the man's chest.

"Oh! Damn woman!! That be hurtin me now!" Hagis yelled.

Mary just smiled, "That oughta teach you not to sneak up on that wild stallion anymore."

After Mary had taken care of Hagis, she brought him a cup of hard liquor and he settled down.

"Drink it now, it will make you feel better." Mary said with a grin. "Thank you, I know it will." Hagis said with a smile.

"Come, sit Lass." said this mountain of a man, "I promise not to bite ye." He told Annie how thieves had ambushed him many years ago and Robert had helped him. "Been friends ever since." Hagis said in a booming voice.

Most of the men who served Robert were loud and vulgar, but they never were disrespectful around Annie or Mary. They knew that if they ever were there would be hell to pay from Master Robert. Hagis was only twenty-six years old but he looked much older, His hair was a dirty brown with red highlights and his full beard was red. His hands were large and his teeth were yellow. The only place that Annie had ever seen anyone like this was in her history books. She was very confused. But one thing she knew for sure: This was not a house being restored. The entire household was something out of the past! Annie started to call Mary's name, but was interrupted by an incessant ringing. What could be ringing? There was nothing here to make such a sound.

Annie awoke and realized she had been dreaming again and the phone was still ringing Annie answered to find it was Rita calling to see why Annie was not at work.

Confused, Annie looked at the clock and saw that it was 8 am. Annie told Rita she was not feeling well and that maybe she should stay in bed for the rest of the day. Rita said that she would inform Annie's supervisor and said that she would check on Annie later.

Annie slipped out of bed, walked into the kitchen, reached into the cabinet and took down tea bags instead of her usual coffee. She only drank tea when she was confused or upset. For some reason she felt lonely and sad, much the same way that she had felt when her parents had died.

"I just need to get away for awhile," Annie said aloud, "I have vacation time due, maybe I should take a few days," she thought. She sat down and slowly sipped her tea. "Yes, that was what I will do."

She cleaned and scrubbed the whole apartment, washed all of her clothes, and washed her sneakers. She realized that she was hungry, so she made a sandwich and poured herself a glass of milk. After lunch, she folded her laundry and put all of the clothes away.

Later, as Annie sat down to watch an afternoon TV show she glanced at the clock on the kitchen wall. It was three o'clock and Rita would be arriving there soon. She turned off the TV, emptied the dishwasher and was just putting the last dish away when Rita knocked at the door. Rita had a large bowl in her hands and was standing in the doorway with a huge grin on her lovely face. When Annie saw Rita holding a bowl she said, "How like you to be so motherly and caring."

"This is chicken soup with garlic just what the doctor ordered," Rita laughed. Rita thought chicken soup cured everything from a runny nose to a broken heart. She only stayed a few minutes, made sure that Annie was okay, then departed. She said she had another "hot date" with Ted and had to hurry home to get ready.

After Rita left, Annie ran a tub of hot water. After a long lingering bath, she put a tape in the VCR and sat down to watch the movie. Rita loved a good comedy and enjoyed the movie, she had not laughed in so long and it felt good. After the movie was over she picked up the tiny kitten and placed it on the bed. It was still too little to jump up by itself. It curled up next to her and fell fast asleep.

Annie felt much better in the morning, but she really didn't feel like her usual self. The days seem to drag by. All she ever did was go to work, came home, watched television and go to bed. Once or twice a week she went out with Bill. Annie had not dreamt for three weeks, and she missed the big, rugged, soft-spoken man of her dreams. She put her nightgown on and went to bed with the little kitten curled up by her neck.

Annie opened her eyes and found that she was sitting under a giant tree near Robert's manor. She heard a loud thundering in the distance and, as it grew louder, she saw Robert riding toward her. She stood and waved, but she could tell that something was not right. Robert was slumped forward on his horse. As he and his men got closer, Annie could see that he was hurt. There was blood on his face and his arm was hanging at an odd angle. How he had stayed on Max no one could have guessed. He couldn't have seen her waving with all of that blood in his eyes. As Max stopped in front of her, and Robert slipped to the ground. Max nudged at Robert's face and pawed at the ground. As Annie approached Robert, she looked up into Max's face and realized that the huge horse looked exhausted, but that he would not have left Robert's side. She reached up and touched Max.

"Robert will be fine," She whispered in Max's ear, "I will take good care of him, I promise."

Annie got some of the men to carry Robert into the house, and then she cleaned his wounds and set his broken arm. The men left and Annie stayed by Robert's side until the sun went down with a flood of bright colors. She walked over to the window and saw Max, still standing in the same spot where she had left him. She went outside and looked at the loyal friend, so visibly tired that he could hardly stand. She took the reins and led Max into the barn.

"I don't know what I'm doing. No biting or kicking, please, just bear with me." Annie was struggling with the reins when John, the stable hand, entered the barn.

"Are you trying to get you bloody self killed!" he shouted.

Startled, Annie turned around, "Oh, I didn't want to bother you. I thought I could handle Max by myself." she said.

"That bloody animal is crazy. Only Master Robert and me kin handle him." John insisted.

"Oh, pooh!" Annie said, "It's about time this horse learned some manners. Just tell me what to do."

John scratched his head, mumbling under his breath. "Unhook the reins on his head. That's the way, lass. Now reach down under his belly…but do it slowly. Don't spook him Unbuckle the strap carefully, now slip the saddle off his back. Take the blanket off the post and rub him down."

As Annie followed instructions, she felt Max's muscles slowly relaxing. She gently led him into his stall after John had lain some fresh hay down.

"Pardon me fur yellin, Miss. Me name is John. I watch o'r the stables fur Master Robert. I was jus' afraid you would be hurt." John spoke roughly but he was really a good, kind man. He had wanted to go out with Robert and the others, but could not. He had ridden in many a battle with Master Robert but, in the last one, his Achilles tendon had been severed and he walked with a limp. Robert told him that they could not chance his battling with such an injury. If they had to go at it hand to hand, John wouldn't stand a chance. So, even though he felt like less of a man, he stayed behind and tended the horses and watched out for the women. He supposed he should be grateful to the Almighty that he could walk at all.

"Damnedest thing I have seen, that crazy horse never let anyone touch him before." he muttered to himself as he walked away. Annie smiled to herself, and then she went back to the house to check on Robert. She wanted to find out where she was and what was happening. Why was everyone so different? Why did everyone talk so strangely? She went upstairs and knocked on his bedroom door.

"Come in." he called. As she entered the room, Robert was moving slowly toward the edge of the bed.

"What do you think you are doing? Get back in that bed" Annie said in her most professional tone of voice. "You need to rest."

"I have to take care of things" he said sternly, only to be given away by the grimace of pain on his face "I can not just lay about."

"Max has been taken care of," Annie said as she gently pushed Robert back on the bed. He just looked at her in disbelief, as though she was crazy, but he was too weak to argue.

"Rest seems like something you could be using too, Miss." Annie turned as Mary came into the room. "I 'ave taken care o' this man all 'is life. He can be very stubborn when 'e wants to you, go on now." Mary gestured at Annie to leave the room.

She had so many questions, and no one could help her but Robert. Annie walked out to the stable, looking for a place to gather her thoughts. She looked in on Max lying in the fresh hay she had always loved horses but had never been up close to one until tonight. Annie went over and sat down next to Max. The hay smelled fresh and clean and Max didn't seem to mind her presence, so she lay back and closed her eyes.

She reached over to touch Max but instead felt a small ball of fur. Startled, she opened her eyes and found herself in her own bed and it was morning. The dream seemed so real; she felt she had really been in another time and place. Annie picked up the kitten and went into the kitchen.

"You smell funny," Annie laughingly said to the kitten. But it was not the kitten that the smell had come from, it was Annie. "How strange, I smell like a barn…like hay or something," she thought.

Annie fed the kitten and then ran herself a warm bath. As she undressed bits of straw fell to the floor. Annie told herself "I *really* have to see that Doctor." She felt like she was losing her mind. It really *was* just a dream, *wasn't it?*

Annie quickly bathed, gave the kitten a pat on the head and went off to work.

She found that Joey was having a good day. He had even gone out on the sun porch for a while. Annie admitted a new patient and then spent most of the day fussing over minor things. She went into Joey's room to tell him she was going home, but found that he had gone home for the weekend. She was happy for him; he needed a break from the routine of the hospital.

On the way home, Annie stopped at the little flea market that was only a short walk from her apartment. "I'll just browse for a while," she said to herself.

She bought a pair of earrings and a couple of flower vases. Leaving the flea market, she stopped at the supermarket. Going down each aisle she realized how difficult it was shopping for one person. Annie knew she only needed a few things, so it did not take very long. She remembered cat food and kitty litter and a small collar.

After putting the food away, she popped a frozen dinner into the microwave. After setting up the litter box for her new pet, she sat down to wait for her dinner to finish cooking. The kitten curled around Annie's feet, making purring sounds. She picked her up and petted her.

She was the cutest little thing. She was mostly white, with small black spots on her nose, left paw and near the tip of her tail. She had the face of an angel.

Annie's thoughts wondered, "I wonder if I would be considered an Old Maid by now? No, I'm too young! Women nowadays get married much later in life" she mumbled to herself.

After making herself a glass of iced tea, she opened her dinner. She put a bowl of cat food down for "Miss Kitty" and sat down to eat her own supper.

Just as she finished her supper the telephone rang. It was Rita and she was just dying to tell Annie about her date with Ted. Most of Annie's evenings ended with a long chat with her dearest friend.

"My, my. What have we here?

Annie jerked upright to see Robert standing over her. He bent down and lifted the kitten up. "Where did this wee creature come from?"

Annie gasped. That was her little kitten in Robert's hand. She smiled, and stood up. "She is mine. I found her by my apartment the other night."

In a puzzled tone Robert asked, "What is a a...part...ment?"

Annie felt that this was the time to find out what was happening to her. "Let's go into the house and talk about it after breakfast."

They walked to the house with the kitten still curled up in Robert's hand. Breakfast consisted of a cold leg of lamb, roast beef, assorted fruits and wine. Annie realized she was very hungry, and she ate more than usual. Maybe it was the fresh air but she felt like a different person. She felt secure and safe, something she had missed for a very long time. She looked at Robert and could see that he seemed to be feeling much better, even his arm had healed.

"Where have you been for the past three weeks?" she asked wondering if she really wanted to know.

Robert set the kitten down and turned to Annie. "A village ta the west was burned and most o' the people were killed or taken." He explained. "James the Terrible has swept across the countryside killing and taking prisoners for too long. I rounded up my men and wiped out a small band of his men to try and teach him a lesson.

"You killed a bunch of men?" asked Annie.

"Aye Lassie." replied Robert. "Women and children are not safe with James raiding the country side."

"How barbaric!" Annie exclaimed, "You just take the law into your own hands? Where are the authorities, the police?" Annie shouted.

Robert looked at her and said,'There you go with those strange words again. What in the hell are these po…lice you talk about?"

Annie knew that this was the time to have that talk that she had planned on having, "Robert, what year is this?" Annie asked.

Puzzled, Robert said, "Lass, don't you know?"

But Annie just glared at him. "Tell me what year this is. Please."

"It is the year thirteen hundred and thirteen, what year do you think it is?"

Annie turned over and opened her eyes. The alarm had not sounded yet, but she was wide-awake.

"Kitty, Kitty, where are you? Breakfast time. Wake up!" She looked under the bed and under the covers, but no kitty. "Miss Kitty" was so little she could be anywhere. "she'll come out when she gets hungry," Annie thought to herself. Before she left the apartment, she left a saucer of milk for her little cat.

When she arrived at the hospital, Annie found that three patients had gone home and a little girl had been admitted. Her name was Kati. She was a pretty little girl, four years old, whose eyes had a look of one much older than she. She had auburn hair that came to just below her jaw line and her eyes were sort of bird's egg blue.

"I'll bet she is a very beautiful child, when she isn't someone's punching bag." thought Annie with anger.

The police had found Kati in a rundown apartment building. She had bruises and what seemed to be cigarette burns on her frail body. She was very malnourished. You could actually see the skin drawn tightly over her tiny bones. Although it was not Annie's job, she bathed her and brushed her thinning hair. The cafeteria sent up hot soup and Jello for Kati and the poor little thing ate like a starving animal. They would have Kati for a couple of days, and then she would be placed in a foster home. After that, if past experience were any teacher, her mother would probably get her back. Annie hoped things would be different this time she hoped Kati would have a chance at real family love, but the chances of that were usually very slim.

Mrs. Abbott, the social worker, came in and talked to the child for a while and then left. When Annie's shift was over, she went in and sat by Kati. "How could anyone be so cruel to a beautiful little girl like this?" thought Annie. "I would give anything to have a child and here is someone that has one and treats her like this. I will never understand this as long as I live!"

A picture formed in Annie's mind of Robert holding the fragile kitten in his large hands. She had never met a man who was so tender and yet so strong at the same time, not since her father. What was she thinking? Robert was just a dream! Could she ever be so lucky as to find a real man like him, the man of her dreams? He was the kind of man that she wanted to be the father of her children. Annie knew in her heart that she would never mistreat one of her own children, and she wanted that same quality in her man.

Walking home after work, Annie felt sad for children like Joey and Kati and yet a warm glow came over her too. She had been thinking about Robert a lot lately and that always produced a warm feeling that she couldn't explain. "Oh, how I wish he was real" she exclaimed out loud to nobody in particular.

As Annie entered her apartment, she noticed right away that the saucer of milk had not been touched. When was the last time that she had seen the kitten? How could it have disappeared so completely and so quickly? The last time was...was...when...No! That made no sense at all. The last time that she had seen the kitten was when Robert had had it in his hands! Her dreams were getting too mixed up in her life. It was becoming too difficult to separate fantasy from reality. "I've got to calm down." She thought.

Annie decided to make a cup of herbal tea. That always seemed to help her relax. As she sipped her tea, Annie surmised that the kitten had found a way to get out of the apartment. She felt a little better telling herself that the kitten would find her way back home, or, at worst, would be taken in by another kind soul.

Suddenly, as her stomach growled, she realized that she had not eaten and decided to fix herself some chicken salad. As she ate her supper and watched the latest news, she thought again about the kitten. The phone rang and it was Rita. They talked and talked until it was time for both of them to get some sleep. Annie got into her bed, missing the softness of the kitten once more. "Damn!" she thought, and a tear rolled down her cheek as she fell asleep.

She awoke feeling refreshed. Thinking she heard a faint meow, she lay very still and listened. She heard nothing but the sound of traffic. The kitten was gone. After her morning ritual, she went to the kitchen and made herself a light breakfast. As Annie drank her coffee she thought of her new patient, Kati. The social worker had said that they would place her in a shelter for abused children in a day or two. Annie knew what the shelters were like. There were too many children and not enough staff to pay attention to each child.

She wanted a family of her own someday, but she knew that she could not manage it with someone like Bill. If she could just find a man like Robert, in real life, it would be perfect.

She cleaned up the breakfast dishes and got ready for work. She was again grateful that she had found a place so close to the hospital so that she could walk to work. As she walked into the hospital she sighed.

"Here goes another day of playing Florence Nightingale," she thought.

Later, after report and rounds, she walked into Kati's room to find that the little girl was in tears. Annie went to her and asked, "What's wrong, honey?"

"I want my Mommy!" the little girl cried, as she cowered in the corner of her bed.

"Your Mommy will be here soon, she is very busy." said Annie "Don't be afraid sweetie, I won't hurt you."

She took a few minutes to sit down on the bed and she held out her arms to Kati. The frightened little girl hesitated. Annie knew not to push it and, after a few seconds, Kati slowly moved into her embrace. After rocking her for a short while, Kati became drowsy and Annie laid her down on the bed and sat there until she was sure that Kati had dozed off.

"Poor little angel," she thought. Annie hated this child's mother she was obviously a woman who had so much yet did not care about anything but herself. Didn't she realize what a blessing a child was this little angel, who had been so badly abused, still loved this creature so much. That was always so hard to understand. Later in the day, Annie checked on the little girl again. She took the time to read to Kati and played a game with her before resuming her other duties.

The remainder of the day was very busy and Annie went home exhausted. She fixed a light supper and sat down to watch "Gone with the Wind." She had put her head on the couch pillows and knew, half way through the movie, that she should get up and go to bed, but she kept watching the movie anyway.

"Hello Lassie." Annie turned to see Robert walking toward her.

"He has the most wonderful smile," she thought to herself. Following close behind Robert was the kitten! The same kitten that Annie had given up for lost!

"Mary has been looking for you, she thought you might like to go into the village for a day of shopping.

"I would like that very much Annie said wondering what kind of shops they had in the village.

"Are you coming with us?" Annie asked.

"Aye," replied Robert, "I have to get a few things for Angus. He is doing some work in the stable and needs some materials."

Robert turned to look at Annie, but she was already walking towards the house.

Annie bolted upright to the ringing of the phone. With a shaky hand, she answered it. Ms. Adams, the night supervisor on pediatrics, was calling to tell Annie that Joey had come back into the hospital and was listed in critical condition. Annie looked at the clock to see that it was only two thirty in the morning. After telling Ms. Adams that she would be right there, she dressed quickly and ran all the way to the hospital.

Joey was lying in his hospital bed looking pale and drawn and he was thrashing in pain. The young LPN on duty, Emma, looked at Annie and said, "He wanted you and no one else." Annie asked for the pain medication and quickly injected it. Very soon thereafter Joey stopped thrashing and was much more relaxed. The shot seemed to have helped him immediately. Annie turned to Joey's parents, Karen and Craig, and said, "He will be okay for the night. You two should go home and get some rest, I will stay with him. I promise to call you right away if he gets any worse."

Annie knew enough about the family to know that they only lived about ten minutes away from the hospital. They were a very close family and she knew that they also had a little girl at home that needed them. Karen and Craig agreed to go home and rest. It was sad to watch them kiss Joey's sleeping face and go down the hall, arm in arm, with slumped shoulders. This was so hard on the families too.

Annie sat by Joey for the rest of the night, thankful that he was no longer in pain. She looked at the dark circles under his eyes and the patches of hair that remained on his head. Soon he would be completely bald and wearing the familiar hat that the other kids wore. Annie looked at her watch and realized that it was almost time for her shift to begin. She walked to the door and glanced back at Joey. He looked so frail and helpless. She had really grown to love this little guy.

As Annie approached the nurse's station, Karen walked up to her with a freshly brewed cup of coffee. "I thought this might hit the spot right about now." said Karen with a slight smile. Annie touched her hand and thanked her.

"Joey is sleeping, they will be up for him later. The doctor wants to do a bone marrow transplant," Annie told her. Karen was grateful because, if it didn't cure him, at least it would give Joey more time…give all of them more time.

After her shift, Annie went home and undressed. Just as she put her feet up, Bill called they made plans to have dinner the following night. She told Bill about Joey and the new patient, Kati. As long as they talked about work, he was very easy to talk to, but Annie was too tired to talk anymore and said goodnight. Bill blew her a kiss and wished her a good night's sleep. After she hung up the phone, she ate a bowl of soup and slipped into her black lace teddy and went to bed.

Chapter 3

Annie looked around, drinking in the beautiful countryside. The mist was so thick that she could not see her feet. The air was damp and chilly. Annie hugged herself, but it did not help. She could smell flowers and clean air and the stillness was wonderful.

"Lassie!" Robert shouted. Annie turned and saw Robert riding up. "Lassie, you are near naked where are your clothes?

As Robert jumped from Max and put his coat around her, she had never seen a man blush such a deep red before. He drew Annie to his chest. She felt her knees go weak and her head was spinning.

Robert bellowed in his thick Scottish accent, "Do you have a desire to die or what."

Before she could answer, he lifted her up on the saddle and got on behind her. Annie leaned against his huge chest and knew she was in love for the first time in her life. Robert was everything she wanted in a man. He was strong, yet gentle and handsome, in a rugged way. She liked the way his dark hair hung around his shoulders (he made the male models of today look like wimps), and the way his crooked eyebrow lifted when he looked at her. His eyes were deep dark chocolate brown and so soft. She even loved the scar that went from his hairline down to his chin.

"I can not let anyone see you like this. Soon the whole village would be talking about my wayward wench! We will sneak in the back door an find you some clothes ta put on."

Annie smiled, he was so old fashioned and it was refreshing to her. As they sat in front of the warm fire drinking a mug of wine, Robert began asking her questions.

"What happened to you? One moment you were here the next you were gone!" he asked.

Annie knew he was referring to the last time she had seen him. How could she explain to him, that she was only with him in her dreams? He would think she was a witch or something. She sat back and began to share her dreams with him, hoping that he would somehow understand. She told him about Boston and how she is a nurse in a large hospital and that she lives in a tiny, two-room apartment. Of course, she then had to explain what a nurse was, and also what a hospital was. There was so much he didn't understand about her world. Robert listened, then touched Annie's lips "Do not ever tell anyone what you have told me. They will surely have you hanged as a witch. I have to think about what you told me. I do not understand any of it." he said and turned away.

Annie caught her breath. "He thinks I am crazy now I have to prove that what I have said is real. But, how?"

Robert told Annie to go on upstairs and that he was going out to the stable to take care of Max.

She slowly walked upstairs and went into her room. There, on the pillow, was the kitten, sound asleep so Annie curled up beside "Miss Kitty", but couldn't sleep. Had she found her true love, only to lose him in a brief moment? No…she would somehow prove to him that she wasn't crazy. A short time later, she tiptoed downstairs to find Robert sitting by the window with his head in his hands. He hadn't heard her decent and she just stood there watching him.

"It will be okay," Annie said to herself, "he will understand someday." She decided not to let him know that she had seen him so she silently accented the stairs and went back to her bed. Annie awoke to hear a rooster crowing and other sounds that she had never heard before. She heard footsteps in the hall and, a moment later, there came a soft knock on her bedroom door. "Miss, Master Robert wants to know if you are all right and if you are ready for something to eat…"

Annie told Mary that she would be down soon…and that she was just fine. She noticed a dress and slippers on a chair near the bed. She quickly dressed, combed her hair and hurried downstairs. Robert looked refreshed yet worried. Annie gently touched his cheek. "Good Morning," she whispered.

He gazed into her eyes and said, "If you are a witch or demented I do not care, I just don't want you to leave again."

"I don't know how to stay, I don't have a choice in the matter let's just make the most of what time we have," Annie said.

"Aye," said Robert, "Let's forget about your other life "an enjoy every moment we have. I have a horse saddled for you I thought we would have a picnic. Mary fixed a basket o' food "an we can spend the day together."

They went outside into the bright sunlight Annie could get used to this smog free air. This period in time knew nothing of pollution and it was refreshing and the smell in the air held little more than the smell of hay and wild flowers. Annie walked over to Max and gave him a kiss on the nose. Robert laughed and said, "Max is a very lucky horse I wish I rated a kiss." Annie turned and said, "All you have to do is ask for one." Robert went to her and took her in his arms. He gently pressed his lips against hers she had never been kissed quite like that before in her entire life. It literally took her breath away! Behind them, Max snorted and pawed the ground, 'someone is jealous," Robert said. Annie smiled and petted Max. "I think you are much more handsome, big boy," she told the huge horse, Robert just laughed.

He walked over and helped Annie onto the little mare. She was not expert at riding, but caught on quickly and was soon doing very well. She drank in the atmosphere all around her, the beautiful hills, and the mist covering the ground and the flowers that grew for as far as you could see. How very beautiful it was here.

After riding for about an hour, Robert dismounted and lowered Annie to the ground. But just as he was taking the picnic basket from his saddle, he heard strange sounds in the distance, like thunder and screams. He grabbed Annie and, literally, threw her on Max. He leapt up behind her and yelled, "Hang on tightly, Lass," and Max took off like a bolt of lightning. The frightened mare ran along behind them...trying desperately to keep up with Max.

Annie glanced behind them and saw a group of men on horseback bearing down on them; they were shouting and swinging long swords in the air. She felt something fly by her arm and then felt Robert slump against her.

"I've been hit Lass, give Max his head and he will get us home." Looking back over her shoulder, she saw dust in the distance and a dozen or more riders coming towards them. All she could do is hold on and pray.

After sometime they came nearer to the manor. Annie was out of breath and Max was snorting and lather was gathering on his neck, but he did not slow down. Several of Robert's men were riding in their direction, because they had heard the thunder of the horse's hooves even from the house. They wheeled around as Max approached and yelled, "Y're doin fine, Lass…follow us!"

Annie was scared to death. This was not a chase scene in some movie…this was for real! After several more minutes (which seemed like hours), it seemed that the others had given up the chase.

"Thank God!" thought Annie, "I don't know how much longer I could have done this."

When they arrived at the house, the men gingerly carried a bleeding Robert inside and laid him on the huge table. An arrow protruded out of his back. Annie ripped his shirt off and examined the wound. Luckily it was not near any vital organs. She ordered the men to boil some water and put the hunting knife in the fire. They tried to tell Annie that they would take care of Master Robert, but she had handled people like this before, so she looked them in the eye and repeated her instructions. They hesitated for a moment, and then rushed off to do her bidding. It had been a long while since she had done her surgical training, but she knew she could handle this. She guessed that they felt that she knew her business, because they all backed off and left Robert to her care.

After cleaning the wound, she took the knife and professionally cut the arrow out of Robert's back. She knew she had to cauterize the wound to stop the bleeding. She put the knife back in the fire, and when it was a brilliant blue she laid it on Robert's skin, counted to four, and removed it. She was so glad that he had passed out…she didn't know if she could have handled hearing his screams of pain. She was relieved when the wound closed perfectly as she lifted the blade.

Annie watched Robert closely for a few minutes, and then instructed the men to carry him upstairs to his bed. After making sure that the wound had not reopened and that he was resting comfortably, she went downstairs to the kitchen to sit down and regain her composure.

Mary rushed up to Annie and asked, "Is M'Lord all right?"

"Yes" Annie assured her, "he will be just fine, although he will be very sore for awhile. I would like to make some fresh soup for him. Is there chicken in the kitchen?"

"Aye Lass, I will get you a chicken," said on of Robert's men, who had been listening from the kitchen doorway. He winked at the other men as he walked outside.

Annie busied herself getting the other ingredients together in the kitchen while she waited for the man to return with the chicken. Moments later the man came in with a live chicken. It squawked and thrashed around as the man held it upside down by its legs. Annie almost screamed, but caught herself in time. She knew he was testing her and she was not about to fail. Controlling her voice she asked if he would mind dressing the chicken while she got everything else ready.

"Don't mind at all Miss." he said as he went back outside shaking his head and smiling.

"I will not let things get to me," Annie said to herself. Within minutes the man was back with the bird all clean and ready to cook. Annie made the soup and took a bowl up to Robert, while Mary gave some to the men who had helped rescue the pair.

"Well, Lass,'Tis good to see you safe. I was worried." Annie found Robert awake and petting the kitten.

"Everything is fine. I took an arrow out of your back. Really Robert, can't you be a bit more careful?" she said jokingly, more in an effort to help her own composure than for his amusement. "I don't think it will get infected. Just to be sure I put a piece of cheese on the wound. Will you have Mary check it tomorrow? Now, I have just what the doctor ordered, Jewish penicillin." she teased.

Now what would that be, pray tell?," asked Robert.

Annie laughed and said, "Good, old fashioned, chicken soup"

"I wondered what that smell was. I do not know how much I can eat though," he said.

She was more than a little pleased when Robert asked for seconds. "I will get fat if you cook very much Lass. Mary is a good woman, but can not cook a'tall."

With a little chuckle, Annie told Robert to rest and she would check on him later. She bent down and kissed him softly and the kitten chose that moment to jump up and lay down by Robert's arm. With a soft smile of contentment, Annie softly closed the door on a drowsy Robert and a sleeping kitten.

She walked out to the stable to see how Max was doing. As she entered the stable she saw the beautiful creature munching on fresh hay. She walked over and gave him a carrot from the bucket near his stall. Max chewed slowly, as if to savor the sweetness of the treat Annie stroked his massive head and talked softly to him.

"Thanks for saving our butts, old friend," she purred.

Max rubbed his nose on her cheek and gave a little neigh it was almost as if he was answering her. John came in to see who was talking he smiled when he saw Annie and walked over and gave her a brush for Max.

"He loves ta be groomed," he said with a smile.

She brushed Max and talked to him about the harrowing day it had been. She could feel his muscles begin to relax. He had grown to trust her. "You must be very tired, my friend you rest and I will sit here for awhile with you. It is so peaceful here that I want to stay forever." Annie said with a sigh.

Annie opened her eyes and realized that the buzzing of the alarm had awakened her. She reached over and pressed the snooze button. What day was it? She had been gone for two days this time, but the clock said differently. It indicated that it had only been nine hours.

It seemed impossible but when she looked at her hands she could see blood on them! It made no sense at all. A person cannot live in two different worlds, hundreds of years apart. It just wasn't possible!

After cleaning up, Annie dressed slowly and walked to work. She found herself worrying about this man called Robert. She felt very confused and bewildered she was so deeply immersed in her thoughts that she had walked right past the front of the hospital. Only when she had to stop for a light at the crosswalk did she realize where she was. Turning around, she retraced her steps and went in to work.

During report, Annie found out that Joey would be getting his bone marrow transplant the next day. The report showed that he was in stable condition, which was a very good sign. He would be in good shape for his transplant. This news excited her greatly and she found it difficult to concentrate on the rest of the cases discussed. She was restless and wanted to get to Joey's room as soon as possible. As soon as report was over, she practically ran to see her favorite patient. There was a stranger talking to Joey when she walked into his room.

"HI', said Joey as Annie came into the room, "come meet James."

She walked over to a tall, good-looking boy, who looked to be around sixteen years old. She had read the history on his medical chart. He was an only child and had been painfully shy until the past year. His mother had died of cancer when he was only eight years old and it had been very hard on him. He had really withdrawn after her death, until his father had remarried two years ago and now he finally felt secure again. His stepmother was a wonderful, loving woman who had drawn James out of his shell and had helped him to build up his self-esteem. "I heard from the doctor that you were a perfect match for Joey," Annie said to this smiling young man.

"Yes, Mam. A nurse spoke to my class about bone marrow transplants and I talked to my parents. We all agreed that it might be a good thing for me to do. I heard about Joey and went right down for the tests. I promised Joey a ride on Thunder when he is well."

"Thunder?" Annie asked. The young man laughed. "My motor bike," he said. "It sounds just like thunder when it's running."

Annie held out her hand. "Well it is a pleasure to know you. I'm Annie Castle, Joey's nurse."

"My name is James Miller. I'm a junior at Glendale Boy's Academy. Sorry, but I have to run. I have a math test tomorrow and I have to study. It was nice to meet you. See you later Joey." James said with a wave.

Annie watched as James walked down the hall. "There is hope for the future after all," she whispered under her breath, as she turned her attention back to Joey.

"Are you going to give me another shot?" Joey asked.

"No sweetie," Annie replied, "I just dropped by to say good night." Annie noticed the fear on Joey's face.

"The operation will make me better, won't it?"

Annie had never lied to him before and she wasn't about to start now. She sat down and took his small hand in hers. "Joey," she said slowly, "we have talked about this before. I told you it does not always work, but that the best doctors are going to give you every chance possible to get better."

"Will you be with me during the operation?" he asked in a tiny voice.

"No, not in the operating room, but I will be here when you wake up. I promise."

She leaned over and kissed his pale cheek as his parents entered the room. She smiled at them as she said goodnight and walked out into the hall. Annie then went down to see Kati; she was wearing a new nightgown and holding a teddy bear, which had been given to her by the staff. The Department of Social Services representative was there to get her; it was all too much for Annie. Kati's eyes would haunt her for a very long time. The social worker had said that she would probably be returned to her mother. Evidently the rights of the mother were more important that a child's safety. She gave Kati a long hug and a kiss and told her to take good care of the teddy bear.

"Have you named your bear yet?"

"Yes! I named it Annie!" replied Kati with a little smile.

Tears sprang to Annie's eyes. She mustn't let Kati see she hugged her again and told her to be a good girl and to come back and visit sometime, and then she turned and quickly walked away. After pausing in the nurse's lounge to get herself back together, Annie went down to ICU and found Rita. "Would you come over to my place for dinner tonight? I want to talk to you about something" she said to Rita.

Rita smiled and said, "Of course."

It was decided that 6:30 would be a good time. Annie had come to the conclusion that she must trust someone with her dreams about Robert. Who would be better than her best and most trusted friend, Rita? The rest of the day went by slowly and rather uneventfully.

Annie prepared a meal consisting of spaghetti and meatballs, garlic bread and a robust red wine. Everything was ready and the table was set when Rita arrived, right on time. After dinner, they sat down in her tiny living room with coffee.

"Okay, spit it out," Rita commanded "I know something is on your mind. Heaven knows you haven't been your usually, attentive self lately. Let me guess, it's Joey. You don't think he is going to make it, do you? Or is it little Kati?"

"While I am really concerned for both of the kids there is something else on my mind." Annie began and then hesitated "I…I really don't know where to begin, but, here goes." She glanced up at the picture of the village, took a deep breath, and began to tell her story.

"I have been having dreams lately that are very real. In fact, they are so real, I am actually there.

"Wait a sec what do you mean, you are actually there?"

"I don't know how to explain it," Annie continued, "I have these dreams and I'm really in 14th century Scotland with a man named Robert, his horse, Max and his housekeeper, Mary."

"Oh my God! A man, a horse and a housekeeper. Wouldn't Freud have a ball with this kettle of fish?" Rita laughed out loud. "I'm sorry honey, but this is a little too much to believe"

"It does sound silly, but I am in this place. Let me explain, I've ridden on Max, seen the countryside, and walked with this man and last night he got shot in the back with an arrow. I had to cut it out with a hunting knife and cauterize the wound." Annie paused, looked straight into Rita's eyes and said, "And Rita, I think I'm falling in love with this man."

"Well, I guess that's one way to get your dream man." quipped Rita. "But, Annie, don't be so serious It's only a dream, you know. You sound like you really think that this is happening. I really think you need a rest, girl."

Annie broke down, hung her head in her hands and started to sob. "I…I…just wanted you to…to know…I had to tell someone. Now you think I'm crazy. Maybe I am!" she wailed.

"No, I don't think you're crazy. Overworked, stressed out, worried about things you have no control over, maybe, but not crazy. Like I said, you really do need a rest. Take a few days off and get out of town, go somewhere and soak up some rays."

"Maybe you're right," Annie said as she began to calm down, "I'll put in for a few days vacation."

"There you go, now you have the idea. Well kiddo," Rita said as she rose, "I gotta run. By the way, is he handsome?"

"What?" Annie asked as she dabbed at her moist eyes.

"I asked if he is handsome, this Robert of yours." "Oh, go on home, you man fiend!" Annie laughed.

"Good night, Annie dear, sweet dreams" Rita laughed as she left the apartment. "Leave it to Rita" Annie said to herself as she shut the door behind her old friend.

Annie loaded the dishwasher and laid out her uniform for the following day. A steady rain had begun to fall. She opened the window in her bedroom and a light breeze came through the room. She was glad that she was on an upper floor, otherwise she wouldn't dream of leaving a window open. That would have been an open invitation for a burglary… or worse.

The combination of the sound of the rain and the breeze was very soothing she looked forward to a good night's sleep. She was careful to wear a more conventional garment to bed as strange as it seemed, she did not want to embarrass herself or anyone else for that matter, if she ended up in that "other world" again.

As it turned out, the night was uneventful. In fact, Annie had what she would consider an uninterrupted night's sleep. The day dawned with cloudless skies and a forecast for nice weather. Regardless of that, Annie had a feeling that something wasn't right. She went through her daily ritual of morning preparation and then went to work. With Kati gone, she had less to worry about, but she still had a very busy day. She ended her shift feeling physically and emotionally drained.

On her way home, she stopped at the store to replenish some of the items she had used up the night before. After paying for her few purchases, she walked out of the store and up to the corner to cross the street. No one knows why she didn't stop to look before stepping off of the curb. If she had, she would have seen the car that hadn't stopped for the red light. All that Annie felt was the searing pain upon impact. She started to scream, but the sound was cut off as the dark world of unconsciousness washed over her.

Doctor Islame was on call in the ER when Annie was brought in. He recognized her, having seen her and spoken with her a few times at the hospital. He knew that she and Rita were close friends, so he sent one of the nurses to find Rita. Then he prepared Annie for surgery. He noted on her chart that she had sustained a concussion, a compound fracture to her right leg and some minor internal injuries. Even though the internal injuries seemed minor, he was going to go in and make sure. Even the minor things had to be repaired and he wanted to make sure that there wasn't anything that he was missing. The fact that she was in a coma was not good. Dr. Islame and a team of others were in surgery for six hours to patch up all the damage. After time in the recovery room to stabilize her, Annie was placed in ICU.

Rita settled down in a chair alongside Annie's bed. Her shift was over, but she didn't want to leave her friend's side. She was not known for strong religious feelings; nonetheless, she bowed her head and offered up a prayer for her best friend.

"Isn't it strange," she thought, "how everyone always looks to God for comfort and help, but only when things are at their worst, never when things are good. We always forget to say thank you, but never forget to yell for help."

Rita wiped a tear from her cheek, took a deep breath, and checked all of Annie's vital signs, which were being monitored by the latest in hospital equipment. As the night wore on everything became quiet, except for the beeps and tones of the electronic monitors.

Robert had his eyes closed and was playing the bagpipes softly like he always did to soothe himself and calm his worried mind. Pausing to adjust his still aching body, he opened his eyes and froze. This was not his beautiful Scotland that lay stretched out before him, but a strange, cold room. Afraid to move a muscle, he sat as still as granite and listened intently. Strange sounds came to his ears. They were totally foreign to anything he had ever heard before He knew something was very wrong. He thought his eyes were playing tricks on him. Without moving, his warrior instincts took over and he silently surveyed his surroundings.

The room was dim, but he could make out the shape of what seemed to be a bed, with someone in it. "It must be a torture rack," he thought as he noticed all the "ropes" and things, which were on and around the bed. From out of nowhere came an unfamiliar, eerie voice.

"Paging Dr. Harper, paging Dr. Harper. Call 317, Dr. Harper, 317 please."

Not even Robert McKenna could sit still for that. He jumped upright against the wall with fear written all over his handsome face. Every muscle in his huge frame was tense and for a few seconds it was quiet, except for the little bells and buzzers he kept hearing. Then he heard a gasp and saw a woman sitting in a chair near the bed. She was starring at him, her eyes wide with fright. The back of her fist seemed to be halfway in her mouth, trying to stifle the scream that wanted to come from her throat.

"What the bloody 'ell is this?" Robert demanded to know, "Who are you?" he said while starring at Rita.

All Rita saw was a very big man, with long hair, wearing strange boots, holding bagpipes, with what seemed to be a skirt wrapped around him. Rita regained her composure long enough to lower her hand and say in a hushed voice, "Robert? Robert, is it really you?

"Aye. It is I. How do you know me, wench?" Robert demanded to know. "It *is* you. You are Annie's Robert," Rita continued in a shocked voice. "Annie?" said Robert, "Do you know my Annie?"

Rita stepped slowly to the side of the bed and switched on the reading lamp, "Annie has been hurt and I've been staying with her, taking care of her," said Rita.

Robert looked at the form lying in the bed. He stepped a little closer, cautiously, it was, indeed his sweet little Annie.

"I do not know why I was brought here but I had a feeling it was because something was amiss." Robert said to Rita. "What happened?" he asked as he moved to take Annie in his arms.

"No! Don't!" Rita warned him, "Don't move her. A car struck her and she just came from surgery, she mustn't be moved."

"Car? Surgery? What strange words are these?" his deep voice was getting louder with each word.

"Quiet, everyone will come running in here if you make a racket." warned Rita.

Robert knelt beside the bed, reaching up and gently moved a strand of hair away from Annie's face, touching her cheek ever so delicately. Speaking in a beautiful Scottish brogue he said, "Come back ta me, Lass. I can not live without you. I want you home with me forever."

Rita walked to the window and looked out, wanting to give Robert a little privacy.

When she turned around, she was shocked again, Robert had disappeared.

She went to the bed and there, on the cover next to Annie's hand, was a leather glove. Rita picked it up and examined it. There was a strange smell like dried blood. She replaced the glove near Annie's hand and sat back down in the chair. Unable to comprehend what had just taken place, she recalled Robert saying a great fear had come into his heart and he was afraid for Annie. He could not explain why he was there, only that he wanted his Annie to come back safe and sound, in his arms.

Chapter 4

Annie recovered quickly, and came out of the coma after twenty-four hours which was a very good sign. Rita came for a visit after Annie was alert and found her sitting on the bed holding Robert's glove.

"HI' Rita said cheerfully, "your dream man is very good looking, but I prefer my men in pants, not skirts."

"Kilts, not skirts." Annie said as in a daze, then suddenly realizing what Rita had said really hit her. "What do you mean my dream man is good looking? You have never seen him!"

Rita sat down and explained, "Oh, yes I have. He popped in for a visit the night of your accident. I was sitting here and all of a sudden there was Robert sitting in the chair by the window. I not only saw him, but we talked, I love his accent." she grinned. "He must have left the glove as a calling card. He said he really needed you and I would say that he cares for you a great deal."

Annie held the glove to her face "I miss him so much. He is what I've waited for all of my life, but I don't see how I can ever have him."

"Stranger things have happened" Rita said, "You never know what can happen when love is in control."

Annie healed swiftly and within a couple of months was back to work. Even though she was able to return to her duties her heart really wasn't in it. She missed Robert terribly. She had not seen him since the accident. She could not help worrying about him, hoping he was okay.

On her first day back to work, after morning report, she went right in to see Joey.

"Well, I see that nurses are human too." Joey said. "I heard about what happened, are you ok?"

Annie walked over, kissed him and whispered, "I'm one hundred percent healthy now, how about a quick game?"

Annie could see that Joey had to finish attaching the paddle device to the new Nintendo game his parents had given him, so she said, "I have a thirty-minute break coming up around two o'clock" she said, "We'll play then, ok?" Joey smiled and agreed.

Annie went back to the desk and heard the other nurses talking in low voices. "What's up?" she asked.

"Oh, you haven't heard yet, that little girl, I believe her name was Kati, was sent back to her mother several weeks ago. Annie, Kati is in ICU with severe head injuries. The doctors don't expect her to live long."

"When was she brought in?" Annie asked frantically.

"Yesterday" Yolanda said, 'she was pretty banged up and is in intensive care for now. The mother said her boyfriend spanked Kati, but no spanking would do the massive injuries that she has."

Annie rushed down to ICU and there, in the third cubicle, laid a tiny, frail Kati. Annie walked over and gasped when she saw the swollen face that lay on the white pillow. Kati's arm was in a cast, half of her hair had been pulled out and both of her lips were busted open. She looked at the EEG machine and saw very little brain activity. Tears welled in Annie's eyes, they were tears of pain and sorrow for little Kati…and tears of anger towards the girl's mother.

"How can people do things like this to innocent children? If she doesn't want this little angel, she should have given her up to someone who does!" thought Annie angrily.

She saw that Kati's teddy bear lay, tore and tattered, next to her right arm. It looked as if someone had attempted to rip it apart sadly, she bent and gently kissed Kati's forehead and left the cubicle.

At two o'clock she went in to play the video game with Joey but he had been taken downstairs for some sort of a test and his room was empty. She left him a note and told him that she would see him the next day. It was just as well, after witnessing Kati's injuries; Annie wasn't in much of a mood to play games.

She thought that the day would never end finally three o'clock arrived and she went home. Gratefully she undressed with a huge sigh, put on her favorite pajamas and sat down with a hot bowl of soup. After a few spoonfuls, Annie went over to the television, selected a channel and sat down to watch a game show.

The scent of fresh hay was all around Annie when she opened her eyes Max snorted and she found herself looking up into the horse's dark brown eyes. "Hello boy, I sure have missed you," Annie said as she stood up and gave Max a hug.

"Well, well, I wondered if I would ever see you again." She turned and Robert was standing in the doorway of the stable. He stood with the sun at his back, his legs apart and his arms crossed, this was the best medicine in the world.

Annie ran into Robert's embrace his strong arms held her firmly but gently for a long while. When she finally pulled back to look up at him, he turned her chin up and very gently kissed her moist lips. After a moment, to savor what had just happened, they walked, hand- in-hand, back to the house and sat by the roaring fire and caught up on the past two months.

Suddenly a scream pierced the air one of the servants came running into the room holding a small boy. The youngster was a stunning shade of blue and Annie could see that he was in real danger.

"My Lord, we were having our evening meal and Ethan grabbed at 'is throat and started to chokin. He can not breathe!" screeched the woman.

Annie grabbed the boy and, placing her fist above his stomach, pressed over and over. Nothing happened, she knew that she had to do something quickly or the boy would die. One more time Annie tried and out popped a chunk of chicken. Just at that moment the boy eyes opened and he sat up what happened he asked, you should not eat so fast Annie told him. She showed him the piece of chicken, this was stuck in your windpipe and you could not breathe.

"Very good Lass. I never me life have seen anything like that""," Robert said with awe in his voice.

Annie couldn't help starring at the child's mother she looked tired and worn as a matter of fact, most of the women that she had seen looked old. The boy's father had been with Robert for ten years and would lay down his life for him, as all the men in Robert's clan would. Annie had a strong feeling that these people would do anything for their Master and

Robert would do everything for them. Let's go out and enjoy the rest of the day Annie whispered in Robert's ear. The weather was beautiful as the sun went down over the mountains, Annie felt like she could spend the rest of her life here. Oh look Annie said pointing to the woods where a large buck and a doe were grazing, she marveled at the nature. They sat down and watched the sun disappear then slowly went in to the house. They sat in front of the fire and Annie filled Robert in on all the things that had happened while they had been apart. Then Robert told Annie about James the terrible raiding the villages and killing so many people.

"Let's forget all the bad things and enjoy the rest of the evening." Annie pleaded.

Soon it was dark and she realized that she was very hungry, her stomach growled and she quickly pressed her hands over it. Robert looked at her and laughed…then they both laughed.

"I'm sure Mary has supper waiting, Lets go on in an make her happy." he said.

After supper, Annie made a mental note that she had to bring more variety to the meals here. The meat was always roasted on an open fire, but vegetables were seldom served. One good thing was that there were never any fried foods.

Robert went to the stable to talk to John and Annie stayed to help Mary the evening passed and soon it was bedtime. Annie retired to her room; she was so tired that she fell asleep as soon as her head touched the pillow.

Annie awoke to the sound of animals instead of cars; she smiled, stretched and realized how much she loved this place in time. Robert had told her yesterday that she could go with him today to visit the people who worked his land for him. She was really looking forward to the trip.

She dressed and went downstairs to find Robert already up, dressed and looking out of the window. Hearing her footsteps, he turned and greeted her with a great bear hug and a kiss.

Smiling at each other, they sat down at the table and Mary brought the food out. The meal consisted of cold pheasant, cold venison, fish beer and bread.

Mary went outside and returned with a bucket, poured some liquid in two cups, and handed them to Robert and Annie. Annie took a tentative sip of the warm liquid. It tasted like milk, but it was thicker and creamier.

"What is this?" she asked.

"Tis goat's milk, Lass," Mary answered.

"It's almost as good as a cup of coffee," Annie said with a smile.

Mary looked at her with a puzzled expression and said "I do not know what coffee is, but thank ye just the same."

Annie got up from the table went to the basin and washed her face and told Robert she was ready to go. She went outside and the little mare was standing beside Max, Annie reached in her pocket took out her watch and put it on her wrist. Robert looked at it and asked what it was, "Oh, this is just a watch," she said it tells you what time it is, why do you need that thing all you have to do is look at the sun. Well I am a city girl and I need it, I can not tell time by the sun as a matter of fact this watch is much better.

Robert looked up at the sun and said, "My time says it would be around 8:00 o'clock in the morning."

Annie glanced at her watch and, sure enough, it was 7:55 a.m.! This man was full of surprises. They got on the horses and started off, rode for about a half an hour and came to a small village. Men, women and children came running out of their huts to greet Robert.

"Any babes born this month?" Robert shouted to the village people.

"Yes, M'Lord, poor Maggie 'ad a cripple, she did. Poor little thing will ne'er walk." said one of the elder women. Annie asked what was wrong with the baby and if she could please see her. Robert nodded and helped her down off of the mare and Annie followed the old woman.

They went into a tiny straw-covered hut to find a newborn baby girl lying in a crudely made cradle. Its mother (a girl that didn't look much older than about thirteen) sat besides her baby, rocking the cradle gently.

Annie asked the young mother if she could look at the baby. She told her that she might be able to help her with the child's problem.

Shyly the young mother said, "Oh, yes Ma'am." and she backed away from the cradle.

"Don't be afraid, I am here to try to help you and your child" said Annie reassuringly.

She picked up the little girl and saw right away just what was wrong. The little girl had been born with club feet. The child's mother started weeping and looked very ashamed.

"I 'ave borne a cripple and I am so ashamed, M'Lord."

Annie looked at Robert and said; "I can fix her feet if the child's mother will let me." "Hush child." Robert said softly. "Miss Annie can fix her, have faith." Robert took the young woman aside and, in hushed whispers, they spoke back and forth for several minutes.

The woman came back to Annie and asked, "Can you really make 'er normal?"

"It will mean you will have to work with your baby every day, but, in time, I believe that she will be able to run and play with the other children," answered Annie with a smile.

"Oh, thank you, Miss! Please, do what you can for her. I will be forever grateful." she cried as she kissed Annie's hand. She turned to Robert and said, "M'Lord, thank you for bringin me an angel."

Annie briskly turned to Robert with instructions. "Please get some leather strips about this wide." She indicated about one inch with her fingers. "Soak them until they are soft."

Robert returned a short time later with the soft leather strips and watched as Annie wrapped them around each tiny foot.

"This will dry and tighten." Annie told the young mother. She explained how each day Maggie was to do this, do not put them on too tight. "In a week I'll come back to see how she is doing" she said.

She touched Maggie's arm gently and they exchanged a smile, then Annie turned and left the hut. She left the village feeling good, with proper care and a mother's touch things would be okay.

They went to a few more villages and the one thing that Annie noticed was that all of these people truly loved Robert, and he really cared for each and every one of them. Annie and Robert arrived back at the manor after eleven o'clock that night. Annie was too tired to eat, so she went straight to bed.

Annie woke early and lay listening to the birds singing their sweet morning song.

"I could stay here forever." she said to herself. This could be a harsh place, but it could also be so very peaceful. She touched the locket that hung around her neck. She had not taken it off since her Dad had given it to her many years ago. She remembered so plainly the Christmas that she had opened the beautiful velvet box and had seen the sterling silver pendent for the first time. Annie remembered her Dad saying how old it was and that his grandparents had told him that it was from ancient Scotland. "How strange it all seems," she thought.

"Lass, are you goin' ta sleep all day?" Robert bellowed.

Annie smiled and jumped out of bed they were going into the village today and they were taking a carriage this time. "I'll be ready in a few minutes, Robert." she called; out dressed quickly and ran downstairs.

After breakfast they went outside and Robert helped her into the carriage they were going to travel for quite a distance, so the carriage was a little more comfortable for this trip. Robert always seemed to be looking out for her.

Annie loved the sights and smells and felt that she would never tire of them. There were so many flowers that she had never seen before and she really liked the heather best of all. She watched Robert driving the carriage and was happy that he had recovered as well as he had from his injuries.

"You seem deep in thought, Lass." Robert said as he looked into her eyes. "Oh yes. I could stay here forever."

"If there is a way for you to stay, we will find it."

"It is so very different in your time," Robert said "I did not like the coldness of your world." Annie knew he was referring to the small room in the hospital where she lay in a coma, and she could not blame him for that observation.

"I liked your friend, Rita." Robert said with a teasing smile. "She seems to care for you a lot."

Annie laughed. "She liked you too. She even said how handsome you were, but she prefers men who wear long pants."

Robert just smiled and shook his head. "One can never figure out women. Well, we are almost there." Ahead Annie could see a small village with shops and animals roaming about.

"Lass, you are as white as a sheep What is it?" he asked as he reigned in the horses.

Annie's eyes were transfixed on what she saw ahead. She had seen this place before, but where? Suddenly she knew. This place looked like the village depicted in her favorite picture, the one on her living room wall! She felt dizzy. She shook herself so she could answer a worried Robert.

"I'm okay now I just feel I've been here before, but that's foolish."

"P'haps ya dreamed about this place?"

"Yes, that must be it." Annie replied with a sigh of relief. "In a dream, I guess." Robert flicked the reins and the horses started moving toward the village again.

As they pulled into the small village, many people waved and shouted greetings to Robert. They stopped in front of a small shop where he was to pick up some items for the horses. Robert helped Annie down from the carriage and told her that she was welcome to look in any of the shops. If she found anything that she wanted all she had to do was tell the shopkeeper and he would put it on Robert's bill. Annie started off to see what was offered in the small village shops after looking in each of the six shops she really didn't see anything she wanted or needed. Shopping here was a far cry from shopping in her world. As she immerged from the last shop, she bumped into a very old woman and almost knocked her down.

"Oh! I am so sorry! Are you okay?" Annie said taking her arm and steadying her.

"Yes, lass I am fine." The old woman looked at Annie. "You look familiar. Do I know you?"

"No, I am a stranger here, just visiting Robert McGregor."

"Aye, I watched you come in to town with him and thought he had taken a bride." the old woman said with a slight smile. Just then Robert came out of the shop he had been in and ran over to Annie. He took her arm and whirled her away from the old woman.

"Be gone with you old woman or I will raise my whip to your back!" he bellowed.

The old woman lowered her eyes and walked away, shocked Annie turned to Robert what was that all about she said between her teeth.

"That old woman has been known to practice witchcraft and you are ta stay clear of do you hear?" warned Robert.

Annie turned to see the old woman watching her from across the street. At that moment she felt a cold chill go down her spine she wanted to talk to the woman, but Robert was leading her away. They went into the shop, which Robert had bolted from just a moment ago, and she waited while he concluded his bartering for the items he needed. After picking out an ox and a cow the couple left the village. As they rode out of town, Annie noticed that the old woman was still there watching her.

"Please tell me more about that old woman, Robert" Annie begged.

Robert's face tightened but he told her that many years ago the old woman had lost her only child to a rival clan when the village was raided. The girl was twelve years old then and the old woman had adored her. After the kidnapping, the old woman had lost her mind and the village people began to think of her as a witch. There was talk of bottles with strange herbs in her hut and there had been deaths that could not be explained. This had always happened when the old woman got angry with someone.

"Do you really believe this nonsense?" Annie asked Robert.

"I have seen things happen that don't make sense." Robert replied. "Enough o' this" he said sternly, "let us get back home and no more talk about the old woman."

Mary had packed a good picnic lunch for them, so Robert stopped under a group of trees and they enjoyed a nice mid-afternoon meal. Clouds started to move in after awhile, so they got everything together to leave.

"Smells like snow's not too far off." Robert said. "It is getting very chilly." Annie said.

Robert reached into the carriage and withdrew a hand-woven blanket. "Mary thinks of everything." he chuckled. As he wrapped it around Annie, she felt a cold shiver run down her back.

"What is wrong, Lass?" asked Robert with concern. He could see that Annie was visibly shaken.

"Something is very wrong." Annie replied, "I'm not sure what, but I feel a need to go back. Something is very wrong." She repeated. "I don't want to leave you again, but…"

Chapter 5

Annie sat bolt upright in her bed, her eyes flying wide open. She got out of bed and was still clinging to Mary's blanket. These were not merely dreams she really did go to the past, she lived in two different worlds, but, obviously, she was needed here now.

Annie got to the hospital to find out that Joey was gravely ill, he had rejected the transplant and there was nothing left to do but wait. Now it was only a matter of weeks or maybe a few months. She sat by Joey for awhile and then went to ICU to check on Kati. She received another shock when she talked to Rita. She learned that Kati was now considered brain dead and that they were preparing to take her off the respirator and let her go home to live with the angels, of which she surely was one.

Annie asked for a few minutes alone with Kati as she gazed down at the child, she became very angry, where was her mother? Why wasn't she here to say goodbye to this sweet child? She lifted Kati (her little frail body had withered to a mere 40 lbs.) out of the bed (being careful of the lines and tubes) and gently rocked her.

Annie thought of her own parents. They had been killed in an automobile accident just before her high school graduation. It had been very hard on her, but she had been raised to be a strong woman and everything had worked out just fine. Rita and the doctor walked in and Annie knew it was time and she looked at the Doctor, may I hold her until the end. The Doctor cleared his throat and nodded Rita wiped her eyes turned and left the room.

When everything was removed, Annie kissed Kati and whispered, "Goodbye angel."

It was over in a matter of seconds and Annie laid Kati on the bed and walked into the sunlight. It had been cold when she was with Robert, but it was late spring here and Annie wanted to be anywhere else but here. She was tired of pain and death, she sat down on a park bench to rest. A strange feeling began to come over her, she felt a ringing in her ears and heard a funny sound. Closing her eyes, she felt a cold wind swirl around her.

Annie found herself in the same group of trees that she and Robert had been in earlier, but Robert was gone. She realized that the sun was going down and she began to get frightened.

"Oh, don't be so silly" she said out loud, "I can surely find my way."

After walking for what seemed like hours, she spotted Robert's huge manor. She saw Max grazing in the open meadow and not far away sat Robert. She watched as he got up and walked over to Max. He looked so forlorn. As he turned to lead the huge horse away, he noticed her standing there with wild flowers at her feet and his face lit up.

"I had to go back because Kati died." Annie explained to him as they walked back to the manor. She told him about Kati being brain dead and how she was by herself and no one should die without a soul there. Annie also told him about Joey and how there was no hope for a recovery; Robert felt maybe this was too much for Annie to handle. She was, indeed, a strong woman but he was still concerned for her emotional well being.

That night Annie went to Robert's bed she needed his arms around her. This is what she had saved herself for.

Annie opened her eyes to the morning light streaming into the bedroom. "I'll be getting the priest today, you brazen hussy." Robert said with a big grin on his face.

"You want to get married?" Annie asked hesitantly, "But how can we when we both live in different times?"

"People will talk if we don't and I won't take no for an answer. So just say yes."

"Oh, I have so much to do. I have to get a dress, fix my hair." Annie stopped, feeling a little sad, "I don't have anyone, any friends or family to be with me."

"Lass, we have each other and we will make our own family, as big as you want!" he said with a smile.

Mary was all smiles as Robert gave orders for the priest to come and all the other stuff that was needed and Mary gave Annie a beautiful long white lace dress. 'This was ta be my wedding gown, but my man was killed in battle, so take it and may it bring you happiness, Lass."

Annie hugged her and with tears in her eyes went off to bathe and dress for her wedding. Everything happened so quickly, the servants fixed Robert's chapel with branches and flowers from outside and everything was lovely. The little chapel was ready in just a couple of hours.

Annie looked around at all the work and love that was everywhere, and Mary was running around, moving things, dusting and giving orders she truly seemed to be in her element. Her weathered face beamed with happiness then when everything was set. Robert knocked on Annie's door and when she opened it she could not believe her eyes.

He looked like a Prince! He was wearing his finest garments. These where the garments he wore when he met with the king. His kilt was made of the finest wool and was a bold Scottish plaid in shades of deep forest green and maroon. He had on a fine white linen shirt with a forest green wool jacket. He wore dark maroon knee-length socks the tassels of green and on his feet were dark brown leather shoes with laces. On his head was a fine beret of forest green with maroon and green trim. He looked like something out of a dream…but he was real this time.

Robert could not take his eyes off of Annie. Her dress was the finest white lace and it had a sheer lace panel from her neck to her bosom and the rest was lines with fine white linen. She wore the pendent under the lace and it fell just where her cleavage would start. She wore heather in her hair, which has now grown to almost shoulder length. Tiny white satin slippers graced her small feet, she was every inch the blushing bride.

A servant appeared, 'The Priest is here and he is ready for You, Master Robert."

The wedding was all that Annie had ever dreamed of. They were piped down the aisle by the most beautiful bagpipe music she had ever heard.

Robert saw a touch of sadness in Annie's eyes and, with his wisdom took her small hands and said, "Y're sainted mother and father are here Lass, you just can't see them. Their love is all around, just close your eyes and you can feel it." Annie did, indeed, feel the love envelop her like the soft mist that lay on the Moors.

The marriage ceremony was like nothing Annie had ever seen and before she knew it she was introduced as Lady McKenna. She looked around at all the food and drink. How had Mary and the others done all of this with such sort notice? Long tables lined the kitchen with meat, fowl, fish, cheese, fruit and large jugs of wine and beer.

As they day grew into evening the wedding reception got noisier and rowdier. Everyone was getting a little drunk and was dancing and cavorting with several of the ladies there. It was great fun and Annie was enjoying herself immensely. Robert drew Annie to him and, like floating on a cloud; they danced around the large room. She looked out of the window just as the first snow began to fall.

"It's a good omen," she whispered in her husband's ear.

"Aye, Lass, we will be happy and have many children." he said with a grin. Annie laughed and said, "Not too many!"

Robert smiled as he swept her across the dance floor to bid everyone goodnight. They spent their wedding night in Robert's room and it was pure heaven for Annie. Their union was everything that sweet dreams are made of, she could not believe how happy she was and how loved she felt.

They arose early the next morning to go away on their honeymoon they planned to go to England. The trip would take a week by horseback, but they had plenty of time and Annie was excited about seeing the pristine forests and abundant wildlife. Robert said that all the beauty she kept exclaiming about held many dangers from wildlife as well as bandits lurking alone the trails. That is why a dozen armed men accompanied them. She could hardly wait to see the castle that he had in England. Annie had never been this happy. Robert was the perfect husband. He was gentle, loving and kind…just as she dreamt he would be.

As they rode along, side-by-side, passing through a port city, Annie marveled at the tall ships in the harbor. She had seen them in history books, but now she could almost touch them. They were grand sailing ships with huge masts that shot up into the clear blue sky like giant fingers pointing to heaven. Perhaps someday they would get a chance to take a trip aboard one such ship. Each time they stopped it was a whole new experience, there was a light snow falling and everything looked so fresh and clean. At night a large fire was built and it kept them warm all night.

When they finally arrived at the castle, Annie could not believe her eyes. It was gigantic! She imagined there had to be at least a hundred rooms. The servants met them at the huge iron gate. Again Annie saw the love and respect that the servants had for Robert. She was introduced to the staff as Lady Ann which made her blush and at the same time proud. The women curtsied to her and the men bowed and kissed her hand. They were all in awe of the woman that had wed their Master and they were very happy to see him so much in love. The days were spent in a whirlwind of trips around Robert's land and shopping, Robert insisted on having gowns hats and slippers made for his new bride. Annie found out she had to have everything specially made there were no shops with dresses on racks or shoe stores. Annie loved the passion filled nights best, she did not like to share Robert with anyone. All too soon they had to return home but Annie knew they would be back.

When they returned home, Mary was standing in the garden, gathering flowers, Robert shouted and waved at her then jumped out of the carriage to give her a great big hug.

"Master Robert, it is so good to have you home, you were missed by everyone. There is a bit of bad news, James has raided a village and has threatened this village. He has said he will have your head on a spear."

Annie shivered at Mary's words. "Not now! Not when things are so perfect," her thoughts cried out.

Robert slowly turned to Annie and said, "Lass, you know what I have to do. You stay here with Mary. I will return to you soon."

Annie wanted to cling to him and beg him not to go, but she knew that she mustn't. She held back the tears as he went into the house and put on his battle gear. He came outside and kissed Annie soundly, got on Max and rode off with his men. Annie kept a straight face until he was out of sight, then she turned to go into the manor. She felt like a cold hand had gripped her heart as tears stung her eyes.

"Please, God, please bring him safely back to my arms," she prayed out loud.

"He is a strong lad" Mary reassured Annie, "He will come back to you alive and well."

Robert was indeed, a strong man and his men were loyal. He would come back to her. Then why was it that she couldn't seem to shake the fear that held her so tightly in it's grasp? She heard the bagpipes fading away in the distance. Robert had told her that in every battle a piper would stand alone and play until the battle was over. The piper was more educated and respected than the fighting warriors.

Annie sat by the window in their bedroom and thought of what her life might be like now. There would be things that she would miss, modern conveniences, like coffee or the hamburger she used to grab at the snack bar. There would be no TV, no tubs of hot water right out of the tap. If she wanted a hot bath, she would have to heat the water herself first. Nevertheless, Annie knew she could be happy leading a simple life here with her beloved Robert. She went down to the kitchen and helped Mary prepare the evening meal. This was something Mary wasn't accustomed to; however she would soon learn to appreciate it.

Sleep didn't come easily that night. Eventually she did fall into a restless night of slumber. When she woke up, vague memories of different dreams she had haunted her mind. After washing her face in the pan of water left in her room, the dream thoughts had vanished. Looking out the window, the sight of new fallen snow greeted her. It wasn't much, but it covered the branches of the trees outside of her window. Down stairs, a blazing fire in the fireplace warmed the great front room.

"Good Morning, Mary, I think I will go into the village and look in the shops today. Would you have a horse readied for me please?"

"I would not go by yourself, Miss," warned Mary.

"Thank you for your concern, Mary, but I am quite capable of going by myself." "Aye, Miss, I will see to it," answered Mary hesitantly.

By the time breakfast was over, the snow had already started to melt and Annie rode into the village and spent some time shopping for a small wedding gift for her new husband. The word had spread into the village and everyone wished the new Lady Annie good luck in her new marriage. Even the old woman carefully approached Annie and wished her well.

Annie remembered Robert's warning words about this old woman, but she seemed so harmless that she talked to her and accepted her good wishes.

After shopping and chatting with the villagers for a few hours, Annie started back to the manor. She had found an exquisite leather vest for Robert. It would look great with his navy plaid kilt and his white shirt.

Upon arriving home, she turned her horse over to John and went into the house, the smell of something wonderful cooking led Annie into the kitchen. Mary was making stew and baking fresh bread.

"My goodness, it smells *wonderful* in here, Mary" Annie exclaimed.

"Thank you M'Lady. How was your shopping trip?" Mary inquired.

"Oh, it was great! By the way, I brought you something." Annie said with a grin.

"Oh my, you didn't have to go and do that!" Mary said with surprise.

"Mary, I wanted to. You are a special person both to me and to Robert. Please open it."

Blushing, Mary opened the box to see a soft, lace nightgown. It was made of a lace imported from France and was the most feminine thing Mary had ever owned (aside from her wedding gown, which she had given to Annie). Tears welled in Mary's eyes as she looked up at Annie.

Annie went to her and embraced her. "You are like another mother to me, Mary, my mother passed away many years ago and I loved her dearly. Please take this as a token of my love."

"I d'nt know what to say M'Lady. I deem it an honor ta be in the same thoughts as your sainted mother, thank you dear." Mary said through her tears, "This is the finest thing anyone has ever given to me."

After having the stew and fresh bread and some wine for dinner, Annie went up to retire for the night. She smiled when she remembered the look on Mary's face as she touched the nightgown. She hoped she was enjoying the feel of the soft fabric against her skin right now. With those happy thoughts she drifted off to sleep.

Annie heard the sound of horses approaching the house. She ran to the window to see Robert riding up. He was okay! She felt her heart leap with joy.

"Thank you, Father" she said as she lifted her eyes to the sky, "Thank You for bringing my love back to me."

She dressed quickly, listening to Robert downstairs talking to Mary and some of his men. As she entered the kitchen she saw him turn and his face was red with fury.

"You are never to go the village alone again" Robert yelled at the top of his lungs.

Taken totally by surprise, Annie squared her shoulders and stood up straighter. "Don't you scream at me, Robert McKenna!" she said with a defiance she didn't know she possessed.

Robert stood silent. No woman had ever talked to him like that before. Looking at this small female with, what seemed like fire in her eyes, he stormed out of the room. Quite shaken, Annie collected her wits and went after him. She found him by the fireplace deep in thought as he turned to her; she threw herself into his arms.

"Lass" Robert said gently, as he pushed her back to look into her eyes, "never go into the village alone again.

"Why?" Annie asked.

"Things are different here, they are not cut and dried like in your time, please listen to me, the old woman is trouble."

Quieting her impulse to argue, Annie agreed. "Alright, I will not go by myself," she said, still puzzled by his outburst but let it rest. The evening meal was slightly strained but turned pleasant; Annie could not stay angry with Robert.

Later, as they sat by the fire, Robert said, "Lass, you need a wee babe ta keep you busy."

If this had been a modern man making this statement, Annie would have been furious, but she was intelligent enough to remember where she was and that he only thought of her. Robert was not being a chauvinist; he was merely trying to find a solution to Annie's loneliness. She smiled to herself, she did want a baby and in the worst way.

"Yes sweetheart, we need to work on that" she said with a wink and a grin. Annie knew that Robert still grieved for his first wife and the son that he had lost so long ago and he would make a wonderful father. She had seen him around the children of the surrounding villages. She remembered the time that they were visiting the tenants of Robert's land. All the children would run up to him and beg for storied. He never turned any of them away. He was such a wonderful man and she loved him so much.

The villages had been unlike anything Annie had ever seen. The houses, or rather huts, were small and shabby and the people were so dirty and impoverished. She had been afraid of getting some kind of disease, but made herself put it out of her mind. They had returned to the village where she had treated the little girl that had been born with clubfeet. Her young mother had been following Annie's instructions and the child was progressing nicely. Annie knew it would take months to straighten the girls" feet but they should be fine.

Again she was amazed at how different things were in this place everything was so unkempt here. The only place that she really felt comfortable was at Robert's…um…*their* manor. Mary was a very clean woman and the manor reflected it. Perhaps, in the future, she could teach the village people some better hygiene.

Chapter 6

Annie didn't sleep well that night. The men were right downstairs, talking loudly about the upcoming battle until the wee hours of the morning. She missed Robert's warmth in the bed as she lay there wondering what might happen to him if James came after him. There were no guns or modern warfare and, most of the time, the men had to fight using hand to hand combat and Robert already had many scars from past battles.

When Robert the Bruce had become king, he had bestowed many favors upon her Robert. They were favors such as land, title and gold. Robert was set for life and didn't have to fight, but he was a man of honor and he vowed to protect his king and his people. The king had also given Robert the castle in England where they had spent their honeymoon. Annie had begun to feel very important being married to Robert. She still blushed, at times, when people referred to her as "Lady Ann."

She awoke early the next morning and realized that Robert had never come to bed. She quickly dressed and hurried down to the kitchen for breakfast. Robert was seated at the kitchen table looking very tired. Mary was bustling about putting food on the table and attempting to clean up the mess that the men had left when they had departed in the early hours before dawn. Robert teased and joked with Annie about the cold lamb and cheese breakfast.

"I would like a breakfast from your kitchen, Lass" he said with a grin. With that Annie got up and went out side gathered several eggs and made Robert a normal breakfast. She sat the plate down and Robert just looked at it, Annie pointed out scrambled eggs, ham, and hash brown potatoes.

"Coffee would make this complete but you will have to settle for milk." she said with a smile.

"What is thing called coffee?"

"Oh, it is a bean that grows in the tropics that you grind and mix with water"

"I will have to think on that." This was what Robert always said about things he did not understand. "I want to spoil you lass, I want to give you everything so I will look into this coffee thing."

"You've already spoiled me." Annie replied as she kissed him softly. "now lets go back to bed for a quick nap." With a wink of the eye, she turned and left the room.

A few hours later they rode out to the country side, Robert wanted to check on his herds of sheep. He told her, as they rode side by side, how he wanted to improve the lifestyle of the people who worked for him. "Most of all, I want a son. I want to teach him to be a good helper of the people, a kind and compassionate man."

Annie saw such love in his eyes when he spoke of children; she silently prayed that she could soon give him what he so desperately wanted. "Tell me about Marion. What was she like?"

Robert did not like to talk about his past, but Annie drew it out of him. "We were young when we met. I had just ended my education and went on to Edinburgh. I saw a redheaded girl and knew she would be me wife. She was buying supplies with her parents. I stopped and struck up a conversation and she asked me to share the evening meal with them and. before long I became part of the family. I don't think I knew her more than two months time before we were wed."

"Five years passed and we had no young ones, but then Marion became with child. She was sick often and had a lot of trouble. When her time came, the midwife came and delivered our son." Robert paused a moment, drew in a deep breath and then continued. "Marion came down with the fever and two days later she died."

He paused again and gazed out across the meadow. "Duncan lived for a week and died. They are both buried over there by that large tree." He pointed toward a grassy knoll and a very large tree across the meadow. "That was where Marion would go and sit for hours, praying for the chance to have a baby. Now they are together forever."

Annie reached across the horses and gently touched his hand. "Thank you for sharing your memories with me. You will have a son again someday, I promise."

Robert turned and looked into Annie's eyes. He stopped the horses and said, "My sweet Annie." He leaned over and took her into his arms and held her tightly to his chest.

"I love you, Lassie" he said gently as he kissed her. "I love you, Robert...so very much."

They rode on for quite some time. There were sheep to be seen clear to the horizon. Annie could see someone on horseback far ahead and as they got closer there were two others on foot as well as two dogs. Robert spoke to the sheep herder as they came up.

"Pull out three hundred and take them to market. And take twenty to the people in the village. They will need them for extra meat with winter here and all." Turning to Annie, he continued, "It is getting late and Mary does not like to hold supper. So I think we should be getting back now. She is set in her ways."

After supper Robert took Annie's small hand in his and led her up the stairs to their bedroom. She paused, looking into his eyes and then reached up and kissed him ever so softly.

"My, aren't we the brazen one now?" Robert laughingly whispered. He swept her up into his arms as easily as a breeze lifting an autumn leaf.

She put her lips to his ear and whispered, "We will make our son tonight."

With the laugh that Annie loved he said, "We are very sure of ourselves are we not?" "Oh yes, my love, I am very sure." she said with a smile.

After Robert fell asleep, Annie slipped out of bed and walked softly to the window. Pulling the curtain back she looked at the fresh snow that had fallen in the hours since their return. From the corner of her eye she saw a doe nibbling at the bits of grass that still poked through the light blanket of snow. Annie watched while the doe eat her fill and then walk into the cover of darkness. With a shiver she realized that she was very cold so she went back to bed. She snuggled close to Robert, causing him to reach for her once more. How she loved the warmth of this man. As

Annie slipped into slumber, she could only think of how perfect her life had become.

She awakened to the morning sun streaming into the bedroom. The space next to her was empty.

"Oh, he must be checking on Max" Annie thought.

She stretched and thought of how wonderful everything was. She lay still listening to the sounds around her and smells drifting up from the kitchen. "Miss Kitty" appeared from nowhere, pouncing on some invisible prey. Annie watched her with amusement. She was surprised at how she demonstrated the great agility and playfulness that only a kitten could display.

Suddenly her happy mood faded as thoughts switched abruptly to Joey. Having rejected the bone marrow transplant, Annie knew that there was not much time left for her little friend. She slipped out of bed and, after dressing, went downstairs. As she entered the kitchen she saw Robert and John sitting with their backs to her.

"We have to put an end to him and his raids." John was saying as she entered. "Good Morning gentlemen" Annie said brightly as she reached for the pot of tea.

Robert stood up with a smile and turning towards her said, "Mornin' Lass." He took her into his arms. John blushed and abruptly excused himself.

"What were you two discussing? Was it about James?" Annie asked. "Not to worry. It is all taken care of." Robert replied.

Annie shrugged and went to get a few eggs and some potatoes and asked Robert to get a slice of ham from the large smokehouse. She made a large breakfast and as usual Robert cleaned his plate and asked for more. Annie liked to cook and take care of him and she felt she wouldn't miss her other life too much.

As the weeks passed and their love grew stronger, Annie often thought of Joey and wondered how he was doing. She awoke one morning feeling very sick to her stomach. She barely made it to the door leading outside.

Robert found Annie there vomiting and he gently held her head. After she had washed her face, she mentally counted backwards. "I'm three weeks late." she said to herself.

Annie went in to Robert and, placing his hand on her stomach. "Say hello to your son."

Robert starred at her in stunned silence. "Are you sure, Lass?" he stammered.

"Oh, yes, I am very sure, my love" she answered with a smile. "I would say you'll be a proud father in the late spring."

"All right, Lass, to bed with you. I do not want you to lift a finger." Robert said with a frown.

Annie laughed and said, "No, no Robert, I am fine and I will have a healthy baby. I know just what to do. I need not lie in bed for nine months!"

Later, as they took their afternoon walk, she felt a strong urge to be close to her husband and she reached out for him. Robert took her hand with a smile. As they sat together under an old gnarled tree, Annie closed her eyes and sighed with contentment.

Hearing strange sounds and smelling strange smells, Annie opened her eyes and realized that she was back in her apartment in Boston. Something must be wrong with Joey. Annie dressed quickly and rushed to the hospital she found Joey slowly slipping away.

"Joey" she whispered softly, "can you hear me?" He opened his eyes and tried to smile.

"Be still sweetheart." Annie said, but Joey moved his lips, trying to speak.

Through parched lips he whispered "I'm not afraid. I will be going home to Jesus soon."

Annie smiled through her tears and replied, "Yes, you are a very brave young man. Jesus will be proud of you, just as we all are."

"I've missed you." Joey whispered. "Your friend, Rita, said you had to go away for awhile."

"Yes, I've been in the country getting better, but I'll stay with you for as long as you want me to."

"Good, I want you to see my angel when she comes down to get me." Puzzled, Annie looked at Karen and Craig with an inquiring look.

"The minister told Joey and his sister that an angel would come down to take him into heaven to be with Jesus when it was time." explained Craig.

"How nice" Annie said, "I hope I get to see her."

The night passed slowly. Joey cried out in pain once and the nurse gave him an injection that worked quickly to ease his discomfort. Everyone wanted to keep him as comfortable as possible.

The sun started rising and Joey opened his eyes.

Grabbing Annie's hand he said, "She's here! She is so beautiful!" He raised his head and looked straight ahead, his eyes wide and his mouth gaping open.

Craig and Karen rushed to his side. Karen took his other hand as he asked, "Do you see her?"

Annie said, "Yes, honey, and she is so pretty. Go to her Joey. Don't worry about us, we will be fine. Go and be happy. We all love you very much."

Sweet little Joey looked at his Mom and Dad and asked in a tiny voice, "May I go with her? Will you tell Amy goodbye for me?"

Holding back the flood of tears they both nodded and kissed him.

Joey held out his arms and gently slipped away. He had gone home to be with Jesus, free at last from the pain and suffering that had gripped him for so long.

Annie grieved with Joey's parents for a few minutes before calling the nurse in to give her the news of his death. She hugged and kissed Karen and Craig and then slowly left the room.

"There is nothing holding me here now." thought Annie. She went out to the little garden beside the hospital and sat gazing at the flowers. Rita would miss her, but she would be just fine. She looked up at the cold morning sky, wondering what Robert was doing at this moment.

"Is he worried about me?" she wondered.

She had to get back to Robert. She had never felt so alone before. Back at her apartment, she sat down on the overstuffed chair, put her head back and closed her eyes. Surprised by a knocking on her door, she sat up. She walked over and looked out the peephole to see Rita standing there. Annie opened the door and let Rita in.

Rita turned to her old friend and said, "It's good to see you, stranger" as she hugged Annie. "I just heard about Joey. I know how close you were to him, so I came by to make sure you were alright."

"Thanks, please come sit down and tell me what's been happening" Annie told Rita. She made coffee while Rita told her that she had covered for her during her absence and had taken care of paying her rent.

"I told your supervisor that you had to get away and rest after your accident. She was very understanding and said for you to take as much time as you need. I've picked up your mail and I've come over here every day to water the plants and make sure everything is okay."

As Annie sat the coffee mug in front of her, Rita said, "Please tell me what's been going on with you."

"So much has happened." Annie sighed, "Robert and I got married and it was the most beautiful thing you could ever imagine."

Rita's eyes grew wide; "You got married to that big hunk?! That's great! Now tell me the truth, you're not really married, are you?"

After assuring Rita that it was all true she went on to tell her about James the Terrible, the people on Robert's estate and about the old woman in the village.

"Well, I see you haven't exactly been bored," said Rita with a grin.

"No, definitely not" answered Annie. "Oh, and one more thing, I'm pregnant!" Rita jumped up with excitement and gathered Annie into a bear hug.

"Annie, I'm so happy for you. I know how much you've always wanted a family."

"You should see Robert. His feet haven't touched the ground since I told him. Can you imagine? He actually wanted me to stay in bed for the rest of the pregnancy. Of course, you know me; I wouldn't have any of that nonsense. But, really, he is so sweet and gentle. He will make a wonderful father," said Annie with a smile. Then her face grew serious.

"What's wrong?" Rita asked with concern.

"I feel that I am there for a reason," said Annie, "I don't know what it is, but strange things have happened."

"Like what?"

"I'm not sure yet. We shall have to wait and see."

"Not to change the subject, but when is Joey's funeral to take place?" asked Rita.

Annie told her it would be the following day. Joey was to be buried at the tiny cemetery on the hill. His parents had bought a lovely spot under a shade tree with a view of the whole city. Joey used to like the twinkling lights at night.

"I hope to go." Annie said.

"I will go with you." Rita said, "You are going to need moral support."

"I appreciate that, Rita. It almost feels like I have lost my own child. I really loved that little guy."

After Rita left, Annie took a hot bath and went to bed. Her thoughts were of Robert. "Please be safe, my love" she whispered to the darkness as she drifted off to sleep.

Annie woke at first dawn and barely made it to the bathroom.

After washing her face, she smiled, "I've always taken you for granted," she said to the small cramped bathroom, "but, never again."

She went to the closet and picked out a nice navy blue suit. She bathed, perhaps for the last time in her bathtub, and had the luxury of a steaming cup of coffee.

Rita came by and picked her up and they went to the church where Annie gazed at Joey for the last time. He had lost so much weight and he looked so frail and small. Her heart ached.

The funeral was very nice, if you can say that about a funeral. Rita and Annie had lunch afterwards. Annie didn't eat much, partly because of the funeral, partly because of her upset tummy.

As they parted, Annie hugged Rita. "What's that for?" Rita asked.

"I have a feeling that I'll never see you again," said Annie with tears in her eyes. "Oh, I will see you again. You can't get rid of me that easy." Rita smiled.

She dropped Annie off at her apartment and watched until she was safely inside.

Annie closed the door and leaned her forehead against it. She stepped back and opened her eyes and was horrified at what lay before her.

Robert's barn was in flames and all of the horses were running loose. Annie ran toward the house to see Robert sitting on the ground with Mary in his arms. Tears streamed down his face.

Annie stopped and asked frantically, "What happened?"

"She was in the barn, getting the horses out and a huge beam fell on her. We just dug her out. She is having trouble breathing."

She knelt down by Mary and took her hand. "I'll make you well," Annie said with tears rolling down her face. Mary motioned for Annie to come closer.

"Go to my room child and look in the chest by the window. Inside is a rolled up bundle, bring it to me, Lass." Mary gasped weakly.

Annie dashed into the manor and found the old chest in Mary's room. In it was a neatly wrapped bundle. She ran back to Mary and gently placed it in her old gnarled hands. Mary opened the bundle. The contents were an old yellowed baby dress and picture. She picked up the picture and handed it to Annie.

Annie couldn't believe what she was seeing. The man in the picture looked just like her father, but how was that possible?

"Who is this?" Robert asked Mary.

"This was my Hamish." Mary said sadly. "I never told anyone, not even you, Robert. Hamish and I were to be wed when he had to go into battle. When I learned he had been killed, I wanted ta die to. It was then that I realized I was going ta have his child. I was only sixteen and me family was disgraced. They sent me off ta England ta a nunnery, where I had the child. The nuns raised her and I came back ta Scotland. Twas a very bad time for my family, so I worked day and night ta help. The years passed and the pain faded. Twas when I found you in that dark hole where your parents hid you, Robert and my life had meaning again. You were such a wee lad and you had nobody ta care for you. Your parents had been killed along with the whole village. I took you and cared for you the best I could. You became a fine man and I am proud of you, my son."

Mary reached up and unhooked the pendant from around her neck. "Please see that me daughter gets this. You will find the address in England where she can be found amongst me things." She looked up at Annie and smiled. "Now you know where the pendant came from." Annie was stunned. She was related to this wonderful woman. This was whom Annie was trying to find all these years.

Mary grabbed Annie's hand and whispered, "Take care of my Robbie. Love him always."

Annie looked up at Robert and they both wept as Mary quietly slipped away.

Robert looked up into Annie's face. "They killed my Mary," he said with a clenched fist. "She never hurt anyone. Mary was the kindest woman there ever was," he cried.

All Annie could do was stand there in stunned silence.

John came over and said, "A few of the horses did not make it, Master Robert."

Annie's heart skipped a beat as she looked around at all of the destruction. Her eyes caught Max's and he walked over to her. She kissed his nose and he walked away.

Annie went to Robert and whispered, "We need to take care of Mary now."

Robert tenderly picked Mary up and carried her over to a grove of trees and laid her down. Annie turned to John and, without a word, he understood.

"Master Robert, let Lady Ann look at your hands an I will care for Mary."

Only then did Annie notice the burns on Robert's hands. Thankfully, they didn't look too bad, so she took him to the house and nursed his burns.

They buried Mary next to Robert's first wife and his son, Duncan.

Robert turned to John and said, "We have to rebuild the barn, then I will take care of James the Terrible." Turning to Annie he said, "I will take you to the castle in England where you will be safe, Lass."

She started to protest but stopped. She knew Robert too well and she knew that it would be fruitless to argue with him. They went back into the manor to pack up for the trip. John loaded the carriage with a trunk and some smaller luggage. Annie climbed up with the precious bundle from Mary tucked into her knapsack.

"Do not worry, M'Lord." John told Robert, "I will handle things here."

Robert knew he could trust his faithful servant. He snapped the reins and pulled away. "How will we get to England?"

Robert smiled and told her that they were going by ship.

"Do you mean one of the ships that we saw on our honeymoon?"
"That's right Lass."

The ride was cold and full of sadness and memories. Robert was deep in thought, some about Mary and other angry thoughts of James the Terrible. As he thought about what Mary had said, he remembered being in the damp hole covered with straw and leaves. The memory suddenly came back to him as if it were yesterday. For a four-year-old boy, it had started as an adventure and then it turned frightfully scary when night had fallen. He had heard the screams of people being killed, but did not comprehend the reality of it. Robert remembered becoming very hungry but he stayed put as his mother had instructed him. He had gotten very cold during the night and had cried. When the sun came up he saw a woman peering down at him. Singing a soft Scottish lullaby, she cradled him and shielded his eyes from the horror that lay all around them.

Robert's life had been good from that moment on. Mary saw to it that he was given the finest education. He learned Latin, French and German and, because of his knowledge, he became a high-ranking officer in the king's army. Mary had been there when he had married Marion and at the birth of his son, Duncan. She had wept with him when he buried his family a short time later. Mary had given up her life for him and he would miss her very deeply. Robert had truly loved Mary.

Annie was sensitive enough to leave Robert alone with his thoughts. She knew how he must have been feeling and when he needed her, she would be there for him.

Chapter 7

When they arrived at the port, their ship was already waiting. They settled into a room and the journey to England soon began. Annie had romantic illusions of what the trip on this gorgeous ship would be like. Those thoughts were soon forgotten.

Shortly after they got out to sea, they ran into a violent storm. The ship tossed and lurched. She was deathly sick throughout the entire trip. This was not the romantic cruise that she had imagined on her ride to the port.

Once, when Robert had gone to speak to the captain, the ship lurched so violently that she had fallen and struck her head on the bureau. Robert had returned to find her unconscious on the floor. He immediately shouted for a doctor. The ship's doctor came running and they transferred Annie to the bed. After a complete examination, the doctor concluded that she had sustained a concussion and must remain in bed for the remainder of the voyage. Robert was very worried about the baby, but was assured by the good doctor that all was well.

Robert fussed over Annie day and night. Even when she snapped at him, he did not take offence. He had more patience than anyone she had ever met. He did wonderful things like bringing her broth and even holding her head when she couldn't keep it down. He gently washed her face and kissed the tears away.

They finally docked in England. Robert took her to an inn for a couple of days so that she could rest and recover from the turbulent sea voyage.

After a few of days of rest, they were on their way to the castle. The journey was done on horseback and would take about three days.

Robert was extremely concerned about Annie riding for that long, but she assured him that she could make it.

Annie was exhausted and looking a little green around the edges by the time the castle came into sight. As usual, the servants were at the gate to greet them. Robert gently helped her off of her mare and carried her down the long hallway to a large, bright, sun-filled bedroom. The huge bed looked very inviting and Annie gratefully crawled under the covers. The woman servant drew the heavy drapes and Annie fell fast asleep.

She did not awaken until evening. She had slept for hours. As her eyes adjusted to the darkness of the room, she could see Robert sitting next to the bed watching her. When he saw that she was awake, he lit the bedside candle.

"You are looking a wee bit better." he said as he walked towards the bed. Annie stretched and announced that she felt very hungry.

"Let me clean up a bit and I will join you downstairs" she said.

"Are you sure you are strong enough to do that, Lassie?" Robert asked with concern. "I will be just fine, love. Go on, I will be down directly."

As it had been on their honeymoon, everything was spotless and she had everything she needed to freshen up and change her clothes. When she walked into the dining room, she could see that the staff had laid out enough food to feed an army. Unfortunately, Annie could barely touch it. She was hungry, but her stomach was still very touchy. One of the women came in with a large tray filled with fruit and cheeses. She did manage to eat some of that (slowly) and keep it down, but she was still feeling nauseous.

"Maybe the morning sickness is finally over." she thought hopefully. Robert had a mug of wine that he handed to her.

"I can't drink wine while I am pregnant, it wouldn't be good for the baby." she said.

"It is alright Lass. I watered it down. It will not hurt the wee babe." he said with a smile, "and it will help you to sleep."

Annie sipped the wine and felt the warmth spreading throughout her body. It actually made her more relaxed and she finally started to feel better.

"I need to stretch my legs." she said.

Robert helped her up and they strolled through the halls of the great castle. Annie had never seen anything so massive. "When we were here on our honeymoon, I didn't get to see much besides our bedroom." she thought as her face flushed.

She took her watch out of her pocket and saw that it was almost midnight.

"You must be exhausted, my love." she said to Robert. "No, Lass, I am fine."

They sat by the huge stone fireplace and Annie told Robert about Joey dying and about saying goodbye to Rita.

"Then you are here to stay?" he asked.

"I think so. I have nothing left in the past. My life is here with you." "I have to leave in the morning." he said sadly.

"You are leaving me here alone already?"

He took her gently into his lap. "You will be fine. The servants will care fur you and you will be safe here. I will return fur you as soon as possible. Rest and get your strength back and I will come to take you back home before know it."

"You're going after James the Terrible, aren't you?" Annie asked fearfully. "Aye Lass, I have to destroy him and his army. I do not have a choice."

She knew better than to try to change his mind. After what they had done to Mary and the manor, Robert would not stop until he and his men defeated that tyrant.

"Please be careful, my beloved, and come back to us." she said as she put Robert's hand on her stomach.

Robert rode off at first light. Annie thought her heart would break as she watched him ride away. While he was gone, she kept busy learning to knit and sew. She learned to make small sweaters and gowns for the baby. She also enjoyed working in the garden and she even took the time to study Latin. She remembered studying it in school and hating it because it was a "dead language" but, in this time period, it was very much alive.

Three months passed and still no sign of Robert. Then one morning, as she was sitting under the giant trees, she saw a horse approaching. It was Robert! She rose and started towards him. It had been so long and she had gotten word that he had been successful in defeating James the Terrible.

As she watched him approach, Annie could see how tired and thin he looked. Oh, but he had never looked better to her. Robert dismounted and gave Annie a gentle bear hug and a passionate kiss.

"I will never leave you again, Lass" he said.

Annie took his hand and placed it on her swollen belly. As if on cue, the baby rolled over and kicked.

"He is a healthy one" she told Robert.

She could see the sparkle come back into his troubled eyes as he felt the baby kick over and over under his hand.

One of the servants ran out to take his mount and they went into the castle. Annie convinced Robert to rest until dinnertime.

Over the evening meal, Robert told Annie about the battle and how his troops faired better than he had expected.

"The manor is almost completely restored." he said with pride. He told her that they would stop and pick up everything she needed on the way home. "There is a new staff, so you will have to start off fresh and train them. We will leave in a week, that will give you time to get things ready."

"You need some sleep." Annie told Robert gently, "come, I'll tuck you in for the night." She got into bed with him, but told him that she wouldn't tolerate anything but being held, not until he got some rest. He pouted and pretended to be angry, but accepted her rules. He held her close to him and whispered his love. It didn't take but about ten minutes and he was out like a light.

Annie waited until he was sleeping soundly and then slipped out of bed.

"It will be so good to get back home" she thought, "I have so much to do before the baby comes."

She put on her robe and slippers and silently closed the door behind her. She wondered the halls and thought of how she had fallen in love with this castle and the people here that had treated her so well. In fact, they had really spoiled her. She would miss exploring the different rooms of this grant castle. She knew that they would be back and that they would be bringing their son with them the next time that they came to visit.

Annie watched Robert regain his strength and fill out in the week that they were there. That week had passed so quickly and now it was time to return home. The carriage was loaded and Robert helped Annie up onto the seat. She turned to wave goodbye and noticed that the servants were dabbing tears away.

The cook came up to her and said, "You bring that young lord or lady back to see us real soon. We will miss your bright, sunny face and your warm laughter, M'Lady."

Annie leaned down and gave the woman a kiss and a quick hug. "We'll bring the baby back as soon as we can, just so you can spoil him." she smiled back.

"God go with you, M'Lady." the cook shouted as they rode off.

The trip back on the ship was much more pleasant then the trip over had been. Annie got to see the beautiful mountains and valleys. The food even tasted good to her and she slept like a baby at night.

The day before they reached land, Robert told Annie that he was ready to get another mare for Max.

"Would you help me pick her out? You have such good sense when it comes to beauty."

"Oh, it will be fun picking out a mare for Max. I think I might know just what he would like." she said with a sly grin.

Robert couldn't help but throw back his head and laugh at his wife. He told her that a large shipment of fine horses was due, so they would have a lot from which to choose.

"Maybe we should get him more than one." Annie teased.

"I don't think so; we don't want to spoil the lad, now would we?" Robert said with a grin.

They soon docked and, as they left their stateroom, Annie heard shouting. She wondered what was happening. When they reached the gangplank, she and Robert saw that there was a near riot in the small town.

"Stay put, Lass." Robert ordered as he rushed toward the madness.

Even though she knew she shouldn't, Annie was not to be left behind, so she followed Robert down the gangplank.

The townspeople had the old woman and they were dragging her towards a large tree. One of the men had a heavy rope in his hands.

"What is going on here?" Robert demanded in a loud, booming voice. One of the men answered, "We are gonna hang us a witch, M'Lord." "What has this woman done?" Robert asked.

"There are no crops and the rains have not come this season. She will put no more curses on this village." the man shouted.

The old woman looked pleadingly at Robert. "Please, Sire, I have done nothing wrong. The people of this village have shunned me for years. The children taunt me and throw things at me when I go by. I am not a witch. Please believe me, Sire." she pleaded. "They burned me house and I have no place to go, so I told these people I would be cursing their crops."

The man who was the leader of the mob spoke up. "The witch spooked a horse and the boy riding him was thrown and killed, M'Lord."

"Sire, the boy was riding by and a wee pup ran in front of the horse. I would not harm a child." she said sadly.

"Did anyone see this pup?" Robert asked in a loud voice. Several of the villagers lowered their heads.

"Well?" Robert bellowed.

"Aye, M'Lord, I saw something." a man said.

Several people throughout the crowd echoed the same answer. Suddenly the group looked very ashamed of what they had almost done.

"You have made this old woman an outcast because she grieved for the loss of a child and because she is different." shouted Robert to the crowd.

With downcast faces the people began to drift away. As the crowd grew thinner the leader walked up to the old woman and said in a low voice, "You had better find yourself some place else to live." and then walked away.

As the man walked away, Robert turned to the old woman and said, "If you need me, you know where to find me."

"Thank ye, M'Lord" she said. She turned and walked toward the remains of her home. She looked so very sad and defeated.

Robert turned and helped Annie up onto the carriage. "We'll be home soon and we can start fresh." As they drove off, Annie turned and saw the old woman standing all alone and waving at her.

"Robert, stop the carriage!" Annie cried, "I will not leave her here alone where she has nothing."

Robert just looked at Annie and said, "What can we do?" he asked.

"Robert, you know I will need help when the baby comes. I would like very much to have the old woman live with us."

"Have you taken leave of your senses, Lass?" exclaimed Robert.

Annie turned to face him and said, "I know what the others think, but I have a sense that that woman is just fine. I am drawn to her and I believe she was meant to help me. Please Robert?"

"Aw, I can't deny you anything, Lassie." he said with a shrug.

They turned the carriage around and stopped in front of the old woman. "What is your name?" asked Robert.

"I am called Lilly." She answered.

"Lilly, me wife has taken a liking to you and she will be needing help with the wee babe. Would you like to be in my service?"

Lilly bowed as graciously as she knew how, "I would be most honored. Would the master mind waiting til I can gather a few things?"

Robert nodded approval. The old woman ran over to a lean-to where she had stashed her meager belongings after the crowd had burned her hut. She picked up a cloth bag, which contained the few clothes that she owned. Robert helped her up into the carriage and they started back to the manor.

The old woman emitted a foul odor.

"Don't these people ever bathe?" Annie wondered.

As always, Robert knew just what Annie was thinking. Laughing, he said to the old woman, "Lilly, you don't know what you have gotten yourself into."

Lilly looked at Robert with a puzzled expression.

"Your Mistress will make you take a bath every day, just like the rest of us." he said. Lilly protested strongly, but Robert held up his hand.

"Save your breath woman. Tis much easier to just agree with my wife."

Lilly smiled at Annie once more and Annie knew everything would be all right.

As they approached the manor, everything looked good again. The new barn was complete and bigger then the previous one. The villagers had done a wonderful job. The only thing missing was Mary. She would surely be missed for a very long time.

Lilly looked at the steam rising out of the bathtub and balked.

Annie tapped her foot and said, "Are you going to get in or do I have to put you in?" The old woman reluctantly took her clothes off and stepped into the hot water. "Good God, M'Lady, do you want me skin to come off?" Lilly shreaked.

Annie handed her a bar of homemade soap and pointed to clean clothes on a nearby chair.

"Scrub yourself from your hair to your toes." she told the woman firmly. She left the room, but could still hear the old woman cursing.

Lilly was actually a nice looking woman once she was clean and had her hair combed. She became indispensable to Annie. She hovered over her and cared for her endlessly.

Annie became bigger and bigger and as time grew near she stayed outside a lot. She couldn't seem to get enough fresh air.

Max had taken to the mare which Annie had selected. Now they were never apart. Perhaps there would be two newborns to look forward to in the spring.

It was a warm spring day when Annie felt the first pain. As she straightened up from the pain, her water broke! She knew that it could take many hours, so she relaxed as much as she could. Soon the pains grew intense and she called for Lilly.

"Get Robert, it is time."

Robert was of no help at first, but soon he did everything that Annie told him. He had worked with Annie for months for this moment. Now that the moment was upon them, he was getting very scared and wanted this to end. After what seemed like an eternity, Annie gave one final push and it was all over. Robert took the tiny baby in his hands and held him up for Annie to see, then handed him over to Lilly.

Lilly tied and cut the cord and placed the baby in Robert's arms. "Oh, Lass, he is so handsome." Robert said with pride.

Annie looked up at her husband and said, "Robert, meet your son, Robert Joseph."

A tear rolled down Robert's cheek as he knelt down beside Annie and said, "Our little Joey."

Annie felt very weak and Lilly had a look of concern on her face. Annie could feel the warm liquid soaking the bed beneath her. Soon it slowed but it did not stop.

She did not sleep well through the night, having nightmares that woke her time and time again. At sunrise she opened her eyes to see Robert and Lilly leaning over the cradle.

"What's wrong with Joey?" Annie cried.

Robert looked at her. "The wee lad has a fever and he whimpers. He is also making a strange gurgling sound in his chest."

Annie knew that her baby probably had pneumonia, but what could she do? There were no antibiotics here and he would surely die without something.

As the day went on the baby only grew worse. At twilight, Annie called out for Rita.

As fate would have it, Rita had decided to go over and check on Annie's apartment. She had not told the landlord that Annie was giving up the place. She didn't know why, but she just couldn't do it just yet.

As she walked around the apartment her gaze fell on the picture on the living room wall. Suddenly it was as if she could feel or hear Annie calling to her from the picture.

"I must be really losing it," thought Rita.

Annie opened her eyes and looked around. She was in the bedroom of her Boston apartment. A sharp pain went through her stomach. She cried out in pain. Her bedroom door opened and there stood Rita.

"Annie! What is going on? How? I…I thought I heard your voice." She continued as she approached the bed. Annie raised her hand and then let it fall. "What is it? What's wrong?"

Annie's voice was very weak as she whispered, "Something is wrong, I delivered a baby boy. We will call him Joey but he is very sick. I need your help. I don't know if I am going to make it. I feel much too weak. Rita," Annie continued, "I need penicillin. The baby has pneumonia."

"Oh no! Ok, I will get whatever you need. I'll be right back. Lie still, you look awful."

Rita rushed back to the hospital and found her newest boyfriend, Anthony, in his last year of residency. She told him she needed a prescription for penicillin, as well as some syringes and sterile water. He hesitated for only a short time before giving her what she wanted. She filled the prescription, obtained the water and rushed back to Annie's apartment. Rita placed the items in a pocket of the gown she was wearing and said, "You know what to do."

Suddenly, Annie gasped and clutched her stomach. Rita pulled back the covers of the bed and said, "Oh my God, you are hemorrhaging." She hurriedly called 911 and the ambulance arrived in a few minutes. The E.M.T. tried to take Annie's pulse but couldn't find it. He couldn't get a blood pressure either. "Transport NOW!!" the man shouted.

As they placed Annie onto the stretcher and rushed her out to the ambulance, Rita heard her whisper, "Robert" very faintly. Annie drew her last breath as they left the apartment. The frantic E.M.T. started to put medication into the I.V. in Annie's arm, but Rita stopped him.

"Let her go, that's what she would have wanted."

Annie was DOA at the hospital. They rushed her into emergency, but what was the use? She was already gone. When Rita looked at her old friend for the last time. She was surprised to see a faint smile on her lips. Rita touched the pockets where she had put the medications and not to surprisingly, found they were empty! Rita walked back to her apartment slowly, knowing that Annie was in the small village not very far from the ocean that she had grown to love so much. Rita smiled at the thought of Robert and Annie so much in love and now their family was complete. Annie was going to make such a good mother. She had waited so long for a husband and baby. Rita went to Annie's apartment to sort through everything and pack it to put in storage. Rita opened the door to Annie's apartment. "Oh, where do I start?" she wondered. She walked into the bedroom, stripped the bed and put everything in the washer. Rita sat down on the bed and looked around the bedroom. "I am going to need a lot of boxes." Funny, she did not feel sad. She knew Annie was not really dead; she had just gone to be with her love. Rita shook her head. She began to look for some boxes and found several in a closet. Annie was always prepared and orderly. Then Rita remembered once a long time ago Annie said that if anything ever happened to her there was a letter in her night stand. Rita opened the drawer and under a lot of papers was a sealed envelope with Rita's name on it. She sat down and opened the letter. The letter was addressed "To Whom It May Concern." There was the name of a lawyer to contact in the event of Annie's death. Rita folded the letter and placed it in her pocket and went to the small living room. How many times had they sat in this room talking and laughing? The room was filled with so many memories. Rita spent the next couple of hours packing and stacking the boxes. The last thing was the picture of the small village in Scotland. "I will have to go there someday and check it out." Rita said to herself.

Rita looked at her watch noting that it was only two thirty. She decided to call the lawyer. The secretary put her right through. The lawyer was very upset to hear the sad news and asked if Rita could come in before five o'clock. She said she would try. Rita looked once more at the boxes and remembered the picture. She went to it and took it off the wall. "This is going with me." Rita went down to the landlady's apartment and told her she would come back tomorrow or the next day to finish the apartment.

The woman dabbed at her eyes, clearly upset. "I will miss Annie so much. She was such a sweet girl."

"Yes, I know. So will I." Rita knew there would have to be some kind of service for Annie. She would take care of that later. Rita started walking and decided she may as well go to the lawyer's office. She did not want to, but knew someone had to. The office was not too far and she arrived there in less then fifteen minutes. It was a one story building on the corner. Rita went in and told the secretary she was there to see Mr. Jordan and sat down to wait. Just as she picked up a magazine, the secretary said "Mr. Jordan will see you now."

Rita went into his office and sat in front of his desk. Mr. Jordan took a folder out and opened it, cleared his throat and said, "Well, Miss Richards, Annie left a substantial amount of money to you with one stipulation." Rita did not answer. "Miss Richards? Did you hear me?"

"Excuse me. Did you say Annie left me money?"

"Yes, and it probably will amount to a little over a million dollars after taxes and fees."

Rita was stunned. She could not believe what she was hearing. "Did you say a…a…million?" barely able to finish.

"Yes, that is correct. But as I said, there is a condition. You must use it to go to medical school."

Tears rolled down Rita's face. Annie knew that being a doctor was always her dream and now she could fulfill it. After Rita answered several other questions and filled out paper work the lawyer said a check would be mailed to her as soon as all the required legal actions were complete.

Rita left still in a state of shock. Annie had done all this two months ago. She knew she would find a way to stay in Robert's time so she took care of Rita. Rita could not get over the fact that Annie thought of her and left her all that money. She felt a big hole in her heart but knew she could fulfill her dreams and make Annie proud.

Annie walked slowly into the bedroom of the manor. She injected the sterile water into the vial of penicillin, shook it, and withdrew the proper amount for Joey. After giving Joey the injection she said, "Our son will be fine now."

Within a week mother and son were both feeling much better. Joey had even been taking milk in the last few days. Time passed, weeks turned into months and months became years. Annie watched little Joey grow to be a fine young lad. He would be their only child, but they were content.

Robert now had a bounce to his walk and Annie was just happy to sit back and watch their child grow. Joey was six now. As Annie stood by the window, she saw Max, the mare, and a new filly grazing serenely in the meadow. She looked over to see Joey chasing Robert around the garden. What a happy, healthy family they had all become. "This is truly what life is all about" Annie thought to herself.

Lilly was a new woman. Caring for this little family was all she wanted. She sat down next to "Mother Lilly" as they all called her now, and watched her two men, with love overflowing in her heart. Joey stopped and waved to the pair.

"Perfect" thought Annie as she put her hand to her throat and felt the pendent there, "Yes, everything is just perfect."

PART 2

Chapter 8

Rita stood waiting to board the plane, eagerly anticipating her trip to Scotland. She had done a lot of research and found a monastery that had records dating back to the fourteenth century. With a little luck they might have information on Robert and Annie and what might have happened to them. It had been seven years since Annie had died and Rita was anxious to know more of the new life Annie had found.

Finally, they called Rita's flight. She picked up her bag and began to merge with other passengers headed toward the doorway to the plane. This was a very big step in her life. She had never been overseas before and she was more than a little nervous, especially after the events of September 11. She had finished her final year of residency and was through with school. Rita found her seat, put her bag in the overhead compartment and sat down breathing a sigh of relief. She put the seat belt on and closed her eyes thinking of the long trip that lay ahead. The plane would land in England where Rita would stay the night then she would take the train to Scotland.

The past few years had been rough. She had to explain to Bill about the way Annie died and answer the never-ending questions that everyone asked. "I think I covered the issue well," Rita thought to herself. Telling Bill that Annie had a one-night stand that resulted in getting pregnant then having a miscarriage seemed to satisfy him. He looked so very sad at the small funeral and Rita felt sorry for him, until he laid his head on his mother's shoulder. Then he just looked to her like a Mama's boy.

Rita went to medical school and went on to become a physician just as Annie wanted. She had not let anything get in the way of her goals. Now seven years later she was ready to open her own practice. Rita had always been poor and she did not know what to think of having several thousand dollars worth of Travelers checks in her purse, but she would now be able to somehow be close to Annie again. She had been corresponding with a monk for several months, who lives in a small village in Scotland. The letter she received said there was a Lord Robert McKenna, his wife and son. The letter did not say much more and Rita was anxious to see what she could find out. Rita ordered a glass of wine and settled back in her seat. Looking out the window, she smiled to herself, "Doctor Rita Richards" it sure sounded good.

Soon the wine and the hum of the plane's engines made Rita drift off into a deep slumber. After a few hours of much needed rest Rita was jolted awake by a jerk, the plane was flying into a lot of turbulence and the flight attendant was telling everyone to make sure their seat belts were fastened. Rita asked how far from England they were she was told they would be landing in a couple of hours.

Rita opened the book she bought and began reading about Scotland; the store clerk had recommended it because of its historical nature. Rita could not believe Annie would prefer this kind of life. Well love does strange things Rita reasoned. Dinner was served and Rita set aside the book until the hotel. After she had eaten she leaned back and gazed out the window thinking about the life Annie had so long ago, was it so much better than life today? Rita closed her eyes and before long they were being told to prepare for landing.

When the plane docked at the gate Rita grabbed her bags and slowly left the plane. She tried to behave as if she was a seasoned traveler but she could not quite pull it off. She was new to this country and it showed. Rita stopped a red cap and asked directions to the underground subway and was soon on her way to Victoria Station. The subway was full and she had to struggle to keep her balance. Before long she was at the beautiful old station. She found a cab and arrived at her hotel within minutes. The hotel was everything she had expected and the room was quite lovely. She took a shower and went down for dinner. It was a little like playing out a fantasy dream, she had heard about things such as kidney pie and other old English dishes, but now it was possible for her to actually partake of these delights. The kidney pie was delicious and the wine hit the spot. After dinner Rita walked around the hotel soaking up all the nostalgia and looking at the beautiful old art that was hanging in the hallways.

Rita stopped in her tracks; a cold chill ran up her spine. In one of the older pictures there was a woman holding a little boy. The woman was the spitting image of Annie. It couldn't be thought Rita; these pictures could have been several hundred years old. But it was Annie, she was sure of that.

Frantically Rita ran to the front desk. The young man looked up, "May I help you?" he asked.

"Yes. Yes. I hope you can." Rita said excitedly "Where did those paintings come from, the one of the woman holding the baby. It's down the hallway on the left."

"I do not know." he said, "but the hotel manager might."

"Please get him now." Rita said with urgency in her voice, "it is very important. I have to know where and when and who did those paintings!" she exclaimed breathlessly.

The desk clerk looked at her for a moment as if to decide what her state of mind might be, then went through the door and came back with a tall, silver haired gentleman that epitomized the English.

"Good evening. I am Charles Madison, the hotel manager. How may I help you?" he asked in a soft distinguished tone.

"Where did you get the painting of the woman and little boy? It's down the hallway on the left." She asked again, this time pointing in the direction she had come from.

Taking control of the excited American as only the English can do, he said, "Let us go and see which one you speak of."

Annie kept just a few steps ahead, almost running and pointing her finger. 'There! There! That one!"

"Hmmm…" he said thoughtfully, "Ah.! Yes. I remember now. That picture came here about twenty years ago. Some rag woman came in with it and another one. It was a picture of a man on a horse as I recall, with a magnificent manor in the background."

"Where is that one?" Rita asked.

"I believe it is in storage. Seems as though I remember there being some restoration needed."

"Would you be able to get it and let me see it?"

"Well I can see what might be done. I cannot promise anything. Let me see what is possible and then I will get back to you. What room are you in?"

"Room two twenty five." she said with a smile. Rita was starting to settle down a little. Looking back at the picture on the wall she asked, "Would you consider selling that one?"

"Do you have an interest in art?" he asked.

"Well, yes I do." Rita said, "And medieval art is the most fascinating."

"You do know your art, not everyone knows that this piece is medieval. As a matter of fact a royal artist around the fourteenth century painted it. So the lady and child must have been very important in that family. If I recall correctly, the other picture in storage was also painted around the same time."

"Why did you say it was not on display with the other portraits?" Rita asked again.

"Well it needs a little repair. It has not stood up to time as well as this one has."

"What would you take for this painting?" Rita asked, trying to hurry things along and not allow the gentleman to begin to think he might take advantage of a situation and ask for too much.

"Well…" he began, "We do sell our paintings from time to time. Let me think about it and I will get back to you."

"That would be fine. Can we see about the other painting now?"

He went down the hall spoke to a lady for some time and returned to Rita. "Mrs. James will bring the painting to your room and I well let you know about the other painting later."

"Thank you."

Rita went to her room to wait. She paced about wondering what the other painting would look like. "Where is that old woman anyway?" she thought. After what seemed like an eternity, a knock sounded at the door. Rita rushed to the door and opened it. Mrs. James stood with a rather large covered painting.

"You wished to see this, mum? She inquired.

"Yes, thank you so much." Rita said reaching for her bag to tip the lady. "Oh, no. You do not need to do that." She said.

"Well thank you very much." Rita said taking the painting. "I will be back later to pick it up." Mrs. James said.

Rita closed the door and uncovered the picture and recognized immediately it was Robert. He was sitting on Max the beautiful horse Annie had told her about. Rita went to the phone and called the manager.

"I will give you ten thousand dollars for both the paintings," she blurted out without thinking when he answered.

"I think that will be sufficient." he said calmly. "I will have the other painting wrapped and brought to you."

"Thank you. I do appreciate that so much. May I ask for one more favor? Could you hold them here for me? I will pick them up when I return from Scotland."

"Yes, Miss Richards. I can do that without any problem. I will have Mrs. James retrieve the other painting from your room later. Will there be anything else?" he asked.

"Not that I can think of right now, thank you." Rita hung up the phone. She could not believe her luck. She had Annie's family right here with her. Rita put the painting aside and went to take a shower. Tomorrow she would leave for Scotland and her trek would begin.

The shower did a world of good for her and she felt renewed. Rita got into bed and did not fall asleep right away. She had so many things on her mind. When she finally did fall asleep, she dreamed about Annie, horses and strange forests.

The alarm went off and Rita groggily got up and dressed and went downstairs for coffee. Mr. Madison saw her when she got off the elevator. "Would you like to join me for breakfast?" he asked.

"Why that would be nice." Rita said.

Over coffee she found out Charles owned and managed the hotel. They talked for an hour and Rita had to get upstairs and get ready to leave for Scotland. As Rita was checking out Charles came out of his office and picked up her baggage and walked her out to the cab.

"Here are a couple of names you might find useful when you arrive in Scotland. They have lived there all their lives and they know everything there is to know."

Rita thanked him again for all his help as she stepped into the cab. She turned and waved as they drove off. He was so helpful Rita thought to herself. This will be a great trip. The train ride was so exciting and the scenery was beautiful.

Chapter 9

Annie worked all day on Joey's birthday party. She had everything but ice cream, which was just one of the things that had not come to pass just yet.

Joey ran into the room, "Mommy, Mommy! When are the other kids coming?" he yelled. "I want the party to start."

"Just be patient a little longer." Annie said, "Everything is almost ready. You want your party to be perfect, don't you?" It took a lot of imagination to do a party for a little boy when you did not have cake mixes and ice cream. Finally everything was ready and the children from the village started streaming in. Robert was right in the middle of things having as much fun as the children were.

"Who wants to ride Max?" Robert shouted. Robert led the children to the pasture and each one had a turn on the ever faithful and trusting horse.

Annie watched her husband with the children, thinking how wonderful the past seven years have been. Robert had gone on trips several times but never for too long. His archenemy James the terrible had not been heard from recently. Soon the party moved back into the house. Everyone sat down to eat. Considering the general wealth of the village, the children were unable to bring presents but there were games to play and much to eat. Before long the children had to leave and Annie sat down to relax. Robert came up and wrapped his arms around her.

"It has been a good day lass, and a very tiring one for you."

Yes the day has passed very quickly and Joey had a lot of fun. Robert helped clean things up and Joey played with the gifts that Robert's men had made. Lilly was fussing around picking up party leftovers and making noises about the loud children and how they can really tear things up.

"I don't guess there will be any need for supper, will there?" she asked Annie. "No Lilly, I think everyone is full and ready to settle down."

Robert and Annie went out on the porch to watch the sun set and relax. "You do not know how happy you have made me lass; since I met you I have never been more content. I have everything I could possibly want and you gave all this to me." he looked deep into Annie's eyes. Annie knew there could never be any more children for Robert and it somehow made her a little sad because he was a wonderful father. Robert looked over at Joey and smiled. The boy had fallen asleep with his head on the saddle that Angus had given him. Annie kissed Joey as Robert cradled him in his arms then carried him upstairs. Robert came back outside and winked at Annie. "Would you like to join me?" Annie took his hand and followed him into the house and to the bedroom.

Annie awoke to the crowing of the rooster and realized Robert was not in bed. She got out of bed and as Annie was dressing she could hear several male voices from the kitchen area. Quickly, she finished dressing and hurried down stairs. When she entered the kitchen she saw three men besides Robert. The room suddenly fell quiet. Annie felt the tension in the air as she gazed into Robert's eyes.

"What is going on?" she whispered. Without a word said, Robert looked at his men and nodded his head toward the door. They all tipped their hats to Annie and filed out of the kitchen into the yard. Turning back to Annie he took her hands in his.

"I have to go to a castle in France. It was my uncle's but he has died and left a lot of things in a mess and I must see how things are because the old castle now falls to me."

Joey came into the kitchen. "Who are those men outside? Are you going away Daddy? Mom, I'm hungry."

Annie smiled at Joey. Just like a little boy, questions and more questions. Annie smiled at him and told him to sit down; it would be just a minute. She also knew better than to argue with Robert on something like this. He had spoken of his uncle, loved him and he had to go. But she did not have to like it. Annie forced a smile for Robert and told him to be safe and hurry home. Lilly had already gotten his things ready so Robert kissed Joey and walked out side with Annie.

"Take care of yourself and Joey. And take care of Max, he is due to be a father anytime now he laughed."

"I will." Annie said softly, "and please do not worry about things here. Just hurry home." Annie watched as Robert and his men rode out of sight. Turning she went back into the house. "Damn, I wish I had a cup of coffee." She thought.

Lilly was fixing Joey's breakfast. "Will Daddy be gone long?" Joey asked. "Yes dear, but don't worry, he will be back home before you know it." Annie had plenty to keep her busy and the days flew by.

Robert had been gone a week when Angus came out of the barn. "Well, Max should feel very proud today. The mare is having the foal."

Annie ran to the barn and sure enough the mare was in hard labor. The time went by quickly and before long the mare was cleaning her newborn filly. Annie made sure the mare and the filly were okay and then went out to see Max. "Well, old boy, you are a Poppa." Annie ran her hand over his velvety nose and down his long neck. "Congratulations! You are a good boy." After kissing his nose she left and went back toward the house. Off in the distance she saw a woman running towards her, screaming.

"Miss Annie! Come quickly! Please! "

"What is wrong?" Annie asked the frantic woman.

"Bess's boy's nose is bleeding and we can not stop it. Please hurry. He has bled so much he is dizzy and very weak." Annie ran to the village and found the boy laying on the ground and his mother beside him crying hysterically. Annie sat the boy up and applied pressure on the side of the nose soon the bleeding stopped.

"He will be fine. Just give him some warm soup and do not let him play for a few days. If it starts again just do what I did and it will stop." As Annie was leaving she noticed a woman looking at her strangely. The woman quickly turned and walked away when Annie gazed back at her. Without giving it much more thought Annie went home. Annie helped with lunch and then sat down and mended several socks for Joey. When she finished the last sock she realized they were out of butter and she and Lilly started churning, Joey loved hot bread and fresh butter. Annie went out to take the clothes off the clothes line that Robert had so expertly hung for her. Annie gathered the dry clothes in her arms and felt a hot breeze brush by her face and looked up towards the west to see dark clouds lingering in the distance.

"Oh damn, we are going to get some bad weather tonight," she thought to herself. Thunderstorms scared Joey and he always ran to their bed and cuddled between Annie and Robert. She missed Robert so much and he had not been gone very long. As she approached the house, she saw Max going to the barn and heard deep rumbling in the distant sky. She almost ran the rest of the way to the house. It was going to be a very loud and noisy night.

Joey was sitting at the table with Lilly. They both turned as Annie came in.

"Did you see the brand new baby?" Joey squealed. "He is so pretty, when can I ride him?"

"You may ride her when she gets a little bigger, now it is time for a reading lesson, then supper and bedtime."

"Okay, but can we read the little book? It is a lot easier and I can read it faster.

Annie smiled. "Yes, you made read that one but you will have to do a few spelling words afterwards. Okay?"

"Okay, but just five words and can I pick them out?"

Annie gave in to his demands and got down to the lessons. Soon darkness covered the valley. Lilly had prepared supper and when they were done, Annie announced the obvious.

"Time for bed," Annie said cheerfully, "put your things away."

Joey took his time but soon things were tidy. "Goodnight Lilly." Joey said as he wrapped his little arms around her neck.

"Goodnight Joey. Sleep well and have happy dreams. I love you."

"I love you too." Joey said as Annie walked upstairs with him. Annie tucked him in bed and returned to the kitchen where Lilly was cleaning up. Annie sat down at the table and sighed deeply.

"Is something bothering you dear?" inquired Lilly. "You look so tired." "I am and I miss Robert, but I miss a lot of other things also."

"What kinds of things do you miss?"

"Well I miss my friends, and other things." She said carefully. "But you have so much to keep you busy here." Lilly said. "And you have so many friends who care for you. You have done so much for the people in the village. They are so much healthier and happier than they were before you came."

Annie walked over to the window. "Yes, I know. I will be better tomorrow. It just takes me a little time to deal with Roberts leaving. I should be used to it by now, but I just cannot do without him."

"Yes and you will be even better when your man gets home again." Lilly said. Annie went outside and watched the lighting move across the night sky, then walked over to the barn to check on the new filly. Everything was quiet. Even Max was settled in for the night so Annie returned to the house. Annie slipped into bed thinking of Robert and fell asleep wondering if he was okay.

Annie slept well and woke refreshed and eager to start the day. After breakfast and cleaning she went outside to work in her beloved garden. Joey played in the yard running over every once in a while to ask questions that only a seven year old could ask. The days went by slowly but thanks to Lilly's company and Annie's daily chores the days were filled with much needed activity.

On one particular boring day Annie was pulling weeds when a man ran up shouting, "Miss Annie! Come quickly! Please. Goodie is having the baby and there is trouble." Annie followed after him as he ran to the village. As they neared the village Annie saw a group of people around a small hut. Annie went inside to find Goodie lying in a pool of blood. Will, her husband, was holding her hand. Annie rushed to the bed and quickly examined the woman only to find the baby was breech and this delivery was not going to be easy. Annie told Will to get a bucket of water and put it on the fire. She turned back to Goodie and in a very firm voice told her to breathe through her mouth. Annie felt someone staring and turned to see that same strange woman she had seen earlier. She was standing in the doorway glaring at her. I will deal with her later Annie thought to herself. Annie had not worked in obstetrics for long but she had seen several breech births and knew she had to turn the baby or she would lose the mother. Annie slowly began to turn the baby until she saw the head present and then she told Goodie to push. After several strong pushes the baby was born. The baby was blue and Annie quickly cut the cord and started CPR. The strange woman still stood with her eyes transfixed on Annie. Annie shouted to Will to bring the water in and to get a bucket of cold water also. Will did just what he was told and Annie dipped the baby first into the warm water then the cold. After several times the baby let out a healthy cry and Annie breathed a huge sigh of relief. She then turned to Goodie and preceded to clean her up, get clean bedclothes on the bed and a clean nightgown on Goodie. Annie stayed with Goodie and Will for several hours to make sure everything was going to be okay. When she got up to leave, Will thanked her for everything.

Annie was very much relieved to see the baby nursing and the healthy pink glow to his skin.

"Take good care of your son." Annie told Will.

"You are a sweet and kind person. How can we ever repay you? If there is ever something I can do for you, please tell me. Thank you." He said. He was visibly shaken. Tears were in the corner of his eyes.

Annie patted his hand. "It's okay, just keep Goodie clean and come get me if anything goes wrong." Annie walked outside and as she passed the old woman, she hissed something at her. Annie stopped and looked at her.

"Witch!" the old woman hissed again. Annie looked at her in disbelief. "What do you mean?"

"I seen you blow into dat wee baby's mouth. What did you do? Blow evil sprits in the poor baby's belly? "

Annie looked long and hard at the wild-eyed woman. "I think it is you who are crazy, old woman." She said and just walked on.

Chapter 10

Rita could hardly believe she was really in Scotland. Now all she had to do was find the monastery that she had corresponded with. The train ride was wonderful and Rita enjoyed every minute. She checked into the Inn and asked for directions to the monastery. She then proceeded to the monastery where she found the old monk she had been writing to over the years. Father Rufus was a small friendly man who was rather pale and shy, but full of knowledge of the medieval history of Scotland. Rita did not tell him about Annie and how she had gone back in time. She had used the ruse of writing a paper about medieval history and wanted to know as much as possible. The monk was happy to talk about ancient Scotland so Rita did not need to pry anything out of him. He told Rita all about Sir Robert and all the travels he undertook and even about his mysterious family. Rita was taken aback when he spoke of the mystery surrounding the family of Robert's.

"What do you mean "Robert's strange family life"?" Rita asked.

"Well, there was not any record of his wife's birth or their son's; it was as if they just appeared out of nowhere. There were strange tales of the "Lady Ann" as he called her, doing strange things and curing the people of the village."

"What kind of strange cures?" Rita asked.

"That I am not really sure of, just the fact she cured people and the mortality rate went down and not as many women died in childbirth." The old monk went on to say that there was an outbreak of something and Lady Ann had had a hand in helping the survival rate. "There is nothing else about Annie after that, there is no telling what happened.

It is pure luck that much was recorded and she was even listed in the records."

"Does it say anymore about Robert and the boy, how old the boy was or anything like that?"

"Well that is just about all there was except that Sir Robert disappeared with the boy and was never heard from again." As the monk poured the tea he continued, "Nothing was written about Annie or what happened and why Robert left with the child."

She thanked the kind monk and went back to the Inn. Supper was an ordeal. Everyone in the dinning room was in a party mood and Rita was in her own private hell.

The days went by slowly and Rita saw a great deal of the countryside.

Everything was so lovely and Rita found herself wanting to stay longer. With only a couple of days left Rita found herself back at the old monastery. Standing outside of the large iron gates, Rita thought, "The father will think I am crazy." She looked at the beauty of the great stonewall that surrounded the rest of the buildings. A path wound through the trees up to the monastery. Lost in her thoughts of how this all looked hundreds of years before when it was first built, she was about to change her mind and was turning to leave when the old monk appeared on the other side of the gate.

"Hello." he said. He then opened the gate and walked up to Rita. "It is good to see you again. How are you feeling today?"

Rita smiled at him and asked if he had a few minutes. "Why of course, come in. There is a bench along the path. We can sit and talk. It is really very quiet and peaceful there"

Rita took a deep breath not knowing exactly what she wanted to say. Again the word "crazy" came to mind but she felt she had to tell someone about Annie. Another deep breath was followed by "I am about to tell you something you will no doubt have a hard time believing, however I don't see that I have another choice."

After she had told the monk the whole story, he leaned back on the bench and looked up at the majestic trees. There were birds singing and squirrels scurrying about. Father Steven spoke very softly. "There was an incident many years ago in a small village some distance from here where several strangely attired men on horse back appeared from the woods carrying cross bows and other strange arms." Rita leaned forward anxious to hear every word. "Their clothing was olden as well. The story as I have heard it repeated tells of kilts and fur boots. The horses were sweaty and lathered as if they had been ridden hard and long. The men were said to be very scruffy looking and dirty. There seemed to be some wounds upon their bodies. The woman who saw them said they acted crazy, yelling and screaming in what seemed to be an old Scottish tongue as they emerged from the forest. They suddenly reined in their mounts and stared in bewilderment at their surroundings as if they were lost. After a few moments they whirled the horses around and rode back the way they had come from and were never seen again. There have been other reports of strange happenings in that area. Once a large fire was seen in the woods at night and the following morning no evidence was found of such a fire. Then there was talk of hearing loud shouts and blood curdling screams emanating from the same area but no one was ever seen or found."

"How long ago was this?" Rita asked. "It was in the late fifties."

"Where can I find this woman?"

"The village is 15 or 20 miles from here, to the north, and her name is... Oh wait; let me think a minute. Yes, yes, her name is Miss Haggerty. She would be in her sixties now if she still lives."

Rita thanked the old monk and returned to her hotel. Since it was still early in the afternoon she arranged for a rental car, checked out of the hotel and after obtaining maps took off for the village the old woman was supposed to live in. Many thoughts ran through her head as she drove. She had to find out as much as she could. Something told her these strange appearances of men on horse back could possibly be connected to the time Annie had gone to. But what did it mean? What kind of a connection? She had to find out. She just had to.

Chapter 11

Annie had a make crude calendar and had the days marked off that Robert had been gone. It had already been a month and she missed him so much. The mare and foal were both doing fine. Max acted very proud and was always around the young horse. He did not stay away from the barn for very long periods of time. It may be hard to imagine a horse acting like a "proud Papa" but that was definitely the way it seemed to Annie. The foal had little white socks just above his hooves. Otherwise he was the spitting image of Max.

Annie enjoyed working in her herb garden and spent a lot of time, with Joey helping, weeding and transplanting different herbs. She had taught the women in the village how to make food taste better with a pinch of this and a touch of that. The men were much happier because the food was not bland and flavorless. Things were so different and relaxed. Annie was learning to do without the things she had before. She walked over to the large shade tree and looked towards the mountains, absorbed in the magnificent and majestic beauty, thinking how lovely the countryside was and how peaceful.

"Mommy." Joey's cry broke her reverie. She turned to see Joey running down the path. He was such a handsome boy. He looked nothing like her for he had all of Robert's features. Annie often thought Joey was a bit too much like Robert. He had no fear of anything, yet could laugh and make others laugh so easily. Annie had taught him well. He could write his name and was learning all his numbers. She was as proud as any mother could me of her only son. "Mommy, lets go see the new pony." Joey continued, as he dragged her towards the barn. The mare was so relaxed with everyone around her filly. She never got upset and let Joey rub and pat the little horse as much as he pleased.

"Come Joey, its time for dinner." Joey planted a big kiss on the mare and waved goodbye as they walked to the house. Lilly had dinner all ready. As they ate she asked if she could go to the village the next day.

"Why of course." Annie said, "I need a few things too. If you would pick them up for me I would appreciate it."

The water was all heated for Joey's bath so all Annie had to do was bathe him and put him to bed. The evenings were the worst time for Annie. Everything was so quiet. She missed Robert so much. Annie and Lilly sat and talked way into the evening. Before long it was time for bed. Annie said good night and went upstairs. Laying in bed she suddenly thought of Rita. "I hope she went to medical school." Annie thought, "I hope she has a happy life."

The bright sun woke Annie. Joey running into the room and jumping on the bed only hastened Annie's rising. Annie and Joey had a leisurely breakfast. After breakfast Annie allowed Joey to go outside and play. Annie had a couple of people to see in the village then she had to do school with Joey. Annie arrived in the village only to find the pregnant woman she had been caring for was out in the field working. Annie very sternly led the woman back to her house scolding her.

"You are due any day now you should not be in the field." The woman reluctantly lay down and let Annie examine her. Annie did not like the way the baby was positioned if he did not turn it would be a breech birth and Annie was not prepared for that. The woman was very run down and not in the best of health anyway and that only complicated things. Annie sat and talked to her and explained how she had to take it easy until the baby came and the woman agreed to do so. Annie knew this baby meant a lot to the woman and her husband because they had lost their other three children in a fire several years ago and they were too old to try again. As Annie was walking back to her home, the husband caught up with her.

"Please ma'm, don't let anything happen to my wife and baby." he begged. "They are all I have."

Annie looked up at this huge rough looking man and noticed he had tears in his eyes. Annie told him she would do everything she could.

"The best thing you could do for her is to insist she gets plenty of rest. She does not need to be working in the fields. You might not only lose the baby but also your wife. Do you understand?" He said he understood and went home in a hurry to check on his wife.

Annie arrived back home to find Joey feeding hay to Max and the both of them looking smug. Joey turned to see his mother approaching. He ran to meet her.

"Mommy, please let me ride Max." he pleaded.

"No!" Annie said. "We have had this talk many times. Your father has told you "No', not until you are bigger. Max is much too big and rough. You can ride Penny. Go and let Angus saddle her for you." Annie was not in a hurry to get down to lessons right now. It would be a good time for Joey to ride for awhile. She was a little worried about the woman in the village. Annie had delivered many babies but this one was going to be a problem. It had her more then a little concerned. The woman was in her late thirties and that was beyond childbearing age in this century. Annie had only her training and wits to guide her. This time that may not be enough.

Max whined as Joey rode by on Penny. Annie waved, "Not too fast!" she shouted.

"Watch, Mommy!" Joey screamed as he took a small jump over a large log.

"Very good." Annie said as her stomach tightened for a second. "Not too fast." she reminded him again.

"Not to worry, ma'am." Angus said as he rode by on his gray mare. "I will look after the lad."

Annie had complete faith in Angus and never had to worry because he treated Joey like his own. They both rode out of sight. Annie went over to the big tree to sit and wait for them. It was times like this she got lonely and wished she could pick up a phone and ask Rita to come over. She got along with the women in the village but had not formed any real close friendships with any of them. Annie shook her head. "Let's not go and get gloomy." she said to herself.

Off in the distance she heard Joey challenging Angus. "I can beat you. Come on. Let's race." Of course Joey always won. In the past, Annie had fussed at Angus, telling him that Joey needed to know defeat if he was to grow into a good and fair man, like his father. It looked like she would have to remind him again. Annie walked towards the woods to keep an eye on Joey as he raced with Angus. He was such a good kid and Annie was very proud of him.

Rita enjoyed the trip even though everything was different and new to her. She got to the old woman's house and found her sitting on the front steps as though she were waiting for her, Rita stepped out of the car, walked up to the very attractive woman.

"Hello. My name is Rita Richards. Father Steven sent me to see you about what you saw many years ago." She said as she extended her hand.

"Ah, yes. You want to know about the strange men I saw come out of the woods over there," she said pointing to a rather large area of trees. "Come inside and have a spot of tea.

"Thank you." Rita said and followed the woman into the house. As the woman poured the tea, she paused and looked out the window. "Can you tell me what it was that you saw?"

"Oh yes. It was a cold clear day and I was going for a walk when I heard the most horrible screaming and loud thunder of horses. I looked and saw three men on horseback riding out of the woods. They were dirty and mean looking and all had swords or bows and arrows and funny looking clothes. The horses were all bigger than any horses I have ever seen before. They all stopped and looked at me. I thought they were going to kill me for sure, but they looked at each other and spoke in a strange language. Then they turned and raced back into the woods."

Rita sat dumbfounded. "Where do you think these men came from?" she paused and then continued, "I mean not so much as where they came from as what time do you think they came from?"

"They did not come from this time that I know for sure, but I do not talk about it any more because people think I am daffy. Some times at night I hear shouts and loud noises come from the woods like a war is being fought but there is no one out there. One time I saw a fire in the woods but the next morning when I went into the woods there was no sign of a fire at all. It is all very strange." The woman got up and walked over to a closet, turned and said, "This is even stranger." Reaching in and taking out a sword she continued her story, "I found this after those men went back in the woods." She held it out to Rita. It looked almost brand new.

Rita took it and almost dropped it, surprised by its weight. "My God, this is heavy. Have you shown this to anyone else?" Rita asked.

"Oh no!" the woman said, "I don't say anything to anyone. But I don't think you think I am crazy."

The sword did not look like anything from this time. Rita certainly was not any kind of expert about weapons, however anyone with a lick of sense could tell that the metal here was not lightweight or stainless steel. The handle seemed to be wrapped with some type of leather strapping. Besides, who would use something like this when guns were the choice of weapons in this modern age? It just looked too crude to be made in this century. She handed it back to the old woman, who put it back in the closet and sat back down.

"You don't think I am daffy. Do you?" she asked.

Rita looked at the woman and shook her head. "No ma'am, I do not think so at all." The two women sat and talked for some time. Rita told the woman about Annie. Not the fact that she had gone back in time but that she had died and how because of her Rita was able to go on to medical school. The woman seemed very happy to just sit and talk. She was evidently very lonely. Rita looked at her watch and realized that she had been there for hours. "I really have to go, but would you allow me to come back and visit again?"

"Oh that would be grand." The woman walked out to the car with Rita. She gazed out toward the forest that was becoming darker as night began to fall. "You know, I wonder sometimes what the world is like where those men came from."

Rita looked out towards the woods and wondered also. "Thank you again, Mrs. Haggerty, so much for the tea and the information. I will be back and stay longer next time.

"I am looking forward to it."

Rita got into her car and watched as the woman went back into the house. As Rita backed the car up, something in the direction of the forest caught her eye. She stopped and looked towards the woods. She stared for the longest time but saw nothing else. What was it she thought she saw? Rita rubbed her eyes and looked again but saw nothing. "I think my imagination is working overtime." Shaking her head in disbelief she began to drive away. She was letting the old woman get to her. It was getting late and the road back to the hotel was a two lane with a lot of hills and curves. "You better pay attention to driving," she said to herself, "or you won't make it back."

Luckily, the kitchen was still open when she got back to the hotel. She enjoyed a delicious dinner and went upstairs to take a hot bath. Rita ran a tub of very hot water and slowly sank into it feeling every muscle in her body relax. She laid back and went over everything that had transpired today. There was a way to go back in time, of that she was sure, but could she do it. She got out of the tub and put her granny gown on and crawled into bed with a thick book. Annie would laugh her butt off if she could see me now, Rita thought. Rita had not been out on a date in ages. She had grown tired of the one-night stands. She worked hard at school and concentrated on it and Annie. Tomorrow she would go driving, look at the countryside and enjoy this beautiful place. Rita knew she could not see the monk for a couple of days because he had gone somewhere for the monastery. Thinking about the day's events and trying to visualize the wooded forest where Mrs. Haggerty saw her horsemen, Rita finally fell asleep.

The next morning Rita slept late and enjoyed a light breakfast she looked through the gift shop picked out a few things that caught her eye. After she put everything in the room she went for a drive.

Rita had been driving through out the area for most of the day. She was enjoying every minute of it. She stopped at a quaint pub for lunch, which consisted of blue cheese soup, trout and a scone and was soon on the road again. She really wanted to go back to the old woman's house and decided she would in the next day or so. Rita saw a wonderful old antique shop as she was leaving the pub. When she walked through the door, the atmosphere seemed to envelop her. She found quiet a few knick- knacks that would look great in her apartment. She also found a beautiful silver tea service that Mrs. Haggerty would really like. Rita did not see any fancy things in the old woman's house so this would be nice. Rita got everything in the car and started back to the inn. She would visit the old woman again tomorrow. Rita wanted a closer look at the area around the house. Hopefully she would be able to find some clue to explain the strange phenomenon Mrs. Haggerty had witnessed. She got back to the inn just as the sun was setting. After putting the things away, she went down to the bar to relax. Rita sat sipping her scotch and soda and thought about the times Annie had described the village Robert lived in and his large manor. If she only had some clue as to its location? Was there a chance she was close to it now? How would she know it if she were? The monk had told her it could be almost anywhere. If she could find the area it was in, perhaps there would be some clue or other evidence, which would show its existence and what might have happened to Robert and Annie. The monk had also said he would look for ancient maps that were stored away. Rita finished her drink and went outside. The little village was unlike anything she had ever seen and she wanted to soak up everything. Some of the buildings looked a couple of hundred years old and the small church looked older than they did. The street was quiet with very few people walking around. Rita looked in the store windows and made a mental note she would have to visit some during the daytime. But for now it was time to go back to the hotel and get some rest.

The telephone woke Rita promptly at seven. She dressed and went downstairs, ordered coffee and planned her day. First she would go back to the Mrs. Haggerty's house. It was a lovely day with warm sunshine and partly cloudy skies. The drive was so delightful, even with the country road; she was there in less than thirty minutes. Rita knocked on the woman's door. There was no immediate response so she waited a few moments and knocked again. "Well, I hope I didn't make the trip for nothing." She thought as she started back to her car. That was when she heard a voice call to her.

"Hello. I am glad to see you again."

Smiling, Rita got out of the car with the brightly wrapped gift. "I hope you will find use for this. It is a tea service." she said, giving the gift to the old woman.

"Oh how sweet of you." she said as she walked toward the house. "Won't you come in? We will put this to use right away."

Rita sat down and visited for awhile. She found out Mrs. Haggerty's first name was Hanna. "You really must call me by my first name, please." she had said. When the tea was finished, she asked if she could go for a walk in the woods behind Hanna's house.

"Are you sure you want to?" Hanna asked. "One never knows when something strange will happen."

"I know, but I still want to look around." Rita went outside and stood looking towards the endless wooded area, then walked up to the edge and stopped. She had no idea what to expect. Hanna had said everyone was terrified of the area and no one ever came near. Rita clenched her fists and walked straight into the woods. Everything was hushed and there was not a hint of a breeze. Rita looked up at the towering trees and felt a calm come over her. Onwards she went, deeper and deeper into the forest. She jumped backwards, as startled as the rabbit that ran across her path. Rita turned and could see the house. "Good," she thought, "I am not lost, yet." She continued walking; soon she was in a large clearing, which was ringed with smaller trees. As Rita bent over to pick a flower she heard something in the distance. Deciding to leave the pretty flower where it was, she walked on. There were sounds and voices that were hard to distinguish. Peering out from behind a bush, she saw a small boy riding a pony coming toward her and could hear him giggling as he shouted "Mommy look at me." The horse with the boy stopped right in front of Rita. The small boy looked straight at Rita, seemingly unable to believe what his eyes were telling him. He was so close she could have reached out and touched him. He shook his head as if to clear this strange vision. But it did not help. He whirled his mount as expertly as any gifted horseman and raced back to the safety of his mother. Rita felt her blood turn to ice when she saw the young woman standing on the other side of the clearing.

"Joey, come in for your lessons."

Rita could not believe what she was looking at. There was no mistaking that voice. The young woman was dressed in a long skirt and peasant style blouse. But, even from this distance there was no doubt in her mind. It was Annie. It had to be Annie. It was really Annie. Rita started walking and shouted, "Annie! Annie!"

The young woman turned and looked straight at Rita. Then, just as suddenly as they had appeared, they were gone. Rita ran still calling for her friend but there was no one there any more. Rita stopped and stood still, gasping for breath; her eyes searched the surrounding area. What happened, she thought. What in the hell is going on here?

"Rita!" Hanna called from somewhere behind her. "Are you alright? What is wrong? Rita! Where are you?"

Rita turned back toward the direction from which she had come. "I am okay. I am over here." She yelled. She started in the direction of Hanna's voice, turning once to back behind her. She had heard Hanna but could not see her through the trees. Entering back into the forest of tall trees, Rita met up with Hanna. Rita's mind was whirling and she still could not talk.

Hanna took her by the arm. "Are you alright?" Rita nodded her head in the affirmative, but did not speak. Together they headed back to the house. When they were inside, Hanna asked, "Who is Annie? I heard you calling for her. I did not know you knew anyone here." Sensing that Rita either could not or would not talk, Hanna decided to stop the questions and just wait for Rita to settle down.

After several minutes Rita found her voice. "May I have something to drink, please?" Hanna brought her a cup of tea. Rita took a sip or two and said, "I thought I saw my friend, Annie, who died seven years ago. I must have been hallucinating. It may have been warmer in the forest then I thought. I felt kind of light headed." Rita told Hanna she had to go back to town. After insisting that Rita sit for awhile first, Hanna walked her out to the car. As Rita was getting in Hanna touched her arm.

"May I ask you a question?

Having regained some of her composure, Rita smiled at Hanna and replied, "Why of course. I'm sorry if I've scared you."

"Oh, that's ok, but this friend, Annie, did she really die or is there something you are not telling me?

Rita looked deep in her eyes. "It's not a long story, but it is a complicated one. Let me just say she died mysteriously. I am really too confused right now to go into it. I truly hope you don't mind. I will say that right now I have the feeling I will be here in Scotland for awhile. I promise you; as soon as I can I will tell you what I know. Now I just need to go back to the hotel and relax. I am sorry and I do hope you understand.

The next time I visit we will have a long talk."

"That's okay dear. I understand. You go on and get some rest. Be careful on the road." Hanna looked very concerned about Rita. "Are you really sure you can drive? You could rest here if you want to."

"I'll be fine." Rita said as she opened the car door. "I'll be in touch soon."

Hanna stood waving after the car until it was out of sight. Rita was still shaken by what she had seen in the woods. "I have to get back here as soon as I can." She told herself as she drove away.

Chapter 12

Annie looked back across the clearing at the large grove of trees. There was no one there now. However, she could swear she had heard some one call her name. "Who called my name?" she wondered. No one lives anywhere in those woods. She thought she saw a slim woman with a tailored look about her, but now she was gone, just disappeared. It still made no sense because no one lives there. The voice sounded familiar but she could not put a face with it.

Joey brought his pony to an abrupt halt and dismounted all in one smooth move. Annie could not help marvel at the degree of horsemen ship he displayed at his age. He ran over to her, breathless and exclaimed, "Did you see that lady mommy? She was dressed funny. She acted like she knew me. Who is she? Where does she live?" It all came out it one continuous stream of words.

"Yes sweetie, I saw her." "Who was she?"

"I don't know, Joey. She was probably lost." Annie said, not wanting to disturb the boy with her confused thoughts. "Now go take care of your pony. And don't waste time in the barn. You still have to do your schoolwork. Now get busy. Go! I will be along in a few minutes."

Joey got back on his pony and started for the barn, "Yes, Mommy." He looked at Annie who was still staring out into the forest. "Are you going in the woods Mommy? Will you be alright?"

"I will be fine. Now you get going." Joey started his mount toward the house and barn. Annie stood still for several seconds and then walked across the clearing to the edge of the woods where she thought the woman had been. She stood still and looked all around but there was nothing there. Annie turned and began to walk back to the house. She had taken several steps when she realized whose voice she had heard. "Oh, my God! That was Rita's voice I heard." she said out loud and whirled around to search the forest again with her eyes. "But that couldn't be. It not possible, is it?" Again, there was no one to be seen. Maybe it is just wishful thinking. She missed Rita a lot and maybe in the back of her mind she just wanted to see or hear Rita. But that doesn't explain who it was. And there was someone there; Joey had seen her too. Whoever it was, she was gone now. When Robert came home again, she would have to ask him about the forest, how deep it was and where it went. For now she had to get home to be sure Joey was doing his schoolwork.

Joey went out to watch Angus in the stable. Annie took the opportunity to go and sit by her self and think. The people in the village had often talked of strange things happening in the woods. Robert had once said some of his father's men had disappeared in the woods for several minutes and when they came back they said crazy things about seeing people dressed funny and strange huts that were not like anything they had ever seen before. Was there a time parallel or something where people could see things that were in the past or future in those woods? Annie tilted her head as she often did when she concentrated and peered into the direction of the woods. It was Rita she had seen. Annie just knew it. And Joey did say she was dressed funny. If she appeared once maybe she will again. Annie got up and walked back to the house. Annie marked off one more day on the calendar and set about making supper. After supper Annie wrote about the week's events. She kept a weekly account in her journal about everything that happened in her life. She wanted to leave it for Joey when he grew up so he would know about her life and where she came from. She kept it well hidden because no one would understand. It could cause a lot of trouble if it wound up in the wrong hands.

Annie washed up after supper and sat down to tell Joey a story before bedtime. After putting Joey down for the night she went out on the porch that Robert had built just for her. Sitting in the rocker that he had also built, she remembered with much fondness the hard work it took in building the porch that was the width of the house. She had laughed and Robert had done a lot of cussing. It seemed to take forever but it was well worth it.

Early the next day Annie went into the village to check on the baby. Joey had begged to go so she took him along. As they entered the village several people were gathered together and that strange old woman was there. She seemed to be in charge. She was waving her arms and talking loudly until she spotted Annie. Then her voice settled to a lower volume. But she still glared at Annie as she and Joey walked by.

"Why is that woman staring at you like that mommy?" Joey asked.

"I don't know honey." was her reply. Some day I will find out, she thought to herself.

Annie checked the baby out and everything was going great. He was nursing and had good color. There definitely was nothing wrong with his vocal cords. Annie was very pleased and told the woman she would be back in a week or so. As Annie was going to the door she turned back to the woman. "Who is that woman talking to the crowd outside?"

The woman looked outside for a moment. "Oh, she is the midwife, until you came. Now she is very upset and is trying to stir up trouble for you by telling every one you are a witch. But most of the village knows you are not, so don't worry your pretty head Miss Annie."

Annie was glad to know the young mother was in her corner. Maybe most of the village felt the same way she did. But Annie could not help the uneasy feeling she had in the pit of her stomach. She did not want any trouble and this woman could make a lot of trouble. Taking Joey's hand in hers, she said thanks and they headed back to the house.

Chapter 13

Rita went back to the hotel, her mind full of troubling thoughts of the events that unfolded that day. It was all like a strange dream. Rita felt like she needed a diversion so she drove into Edinburgh. She was not sure what she wanted to do so she started walking down the main street just looking at all the department stores. Rita went into a fancy dress shop and browsed. Nothing peaked her interest so she left. She spotted a shoe store and found a lovely pair of shoes. She bough them and headed back to the hotel. When she got to the hotel see realized it was almost dinnertime but just went to her room and ordered a bowl of soup. After turning on the television, she remained in her room trying to sort things out. If there were a connection with this *time thing* then it would be necessary to act quickly. Rita recalled the monk saying the boy Joey was about eight or nine when those events took place and the Joey she saw in the woods was at least six or seven. Rita finally dozed off. In a fitful sleep, she dreamed of Annie calling for help and looking right at Rita but she could not get to her to help.

Rita got up early the next morning and set off for the monastery. She was determined to get all the information she could. Rita knew she had to do something, what she was not sure of but she would find a way to fix things. The old monk was only too happy to assist Rita getting out the old record books. They looked like they were about to fall apart. Rita spent hours going through the books finally finding several references of health care and other related items. Rita pointed this out to the monk and he only said that the village did have a lower mortality rate than other villages around.

"Do you believe the story that Hanna saw warriors come out of the woods?"

Without hesitating the monk said, "Yes. I do feel there was validity in the story." The monk went on to say there have been a lot of strange things that have happened in his lifetime and stranger things have happened. Rita thanked the monk for all his help. He walked her out to her car. Rita told him about the encounter in the woods with Annie and Joey. The monk stopped in his tracks and turned to her with a strange look on his face. "This is very interesting. Not only has someone from the past come through this passage. It seems perhaps one can go back in time as well."

"Do you really feel that someone can cross time?" Rita asked.

"Is anything really impossible?" the monk said looking out over the rolling hills in the distance. "I have seen and heard of a lot of strange things and do not doubt some wondrous things do occur."

She knew she could not return to the states. Why, she was not to sure, but something inside told her she had to stay.

Chapter 14

Things were bad enough not knowing where James the Terrible was, or what he was up to. The country was so unstable at times it would be just like James to use an opportunity like this to go on a rampage again. Annie wanted Robert home again to comfort her and make things safe. Annie walked over to the window and gazed out, "Oh damn!" Annie said out loud. It was raining again. It had rained for days and Joey was getting cabin fever. She took the homemade checkers game out. They always had fun playing games. They had played several games when suddenly a very bright bolt of lightening was followed immediately by an extremely loud clap of thunder. The weather got really bad and Annie grew more nervous. The lightening was so close she could see the glowing bolts flashing from the sky to the ground. Joey seemed to lose interest in the checkers and kept staring at the window.

"Are you scared, honey?" "A little."

"Well there is nothing to be afraid of. It will pass over soon. Come on lets get you to bed. By the time you are in bed it will be gone." She hoped her optimism turned out to be prophetic.

Annie took him upstairs and put him to bed. The storm did seem to be fading. It was still raining but the awesome thunder and frequent lightening were subsiding.

'See? I told you it would get better."

Annie sat on the bed until Joey fell into a fitful slumber. She kissed his head and turned to leave the room. As if to test her resolve, the storm emitted one more brilliant flash of lightening. It lit up the room as well as the surrounding woods. Annie was looking toward the window at the moment and thought she saw a rider coming out of the woods, galloping at full speed towards the barn. She turned to check on Joey. He was sound asleep now, totally oblivious to the latest flash. She hurried downstairs and went to the front door. Opening it up, she strained to see through the blinding rain. Annie stood frozen in the doorway, praying it would be Robert returning.

Another distant bolt allowed Annie to see Angus coming out of the barn. He was carrying a lantern. The horseman slowed as he approached Angus. In the dim glow of the lantern, she saw the figure dismount and they disappeared into the dark barn. She kept hoping and praying it was Robert. After a few minutes a figure emerged and ran toward the house. It was indeed Robert and he was soaking wet. Annie helped him to the chair by the fireplace.

She put a blanket over his shoulders and ran to get Lilly. While Lilly was heating up soup Annie went back to Robert.

"Why the big fuss? I am not dying. I am just wet" he laughed.

Annie stopped and smiled. Yes. Everything was back to normal. Everything was as it should be and the house would be full of laughter again.

Annie and Robert walked upstairs, and checked on Joey who was sound asleep Robert went over and kissed him stood looking at the boy for a minute then turned and went back to Annie. They went down the hall to their room and as they were getting ready for bed Annie turned to Robert.

"You were gone so long. What all did you do and where did you go?"

"You are so full of questions. Can't I have a few secrets?"

"What do you mean?"

"Oh no, you don't get any more out of me tonight. Come over here and show me how much you missed me."

Annie ran to him and they fell on the bed, but before she went to sleep she asked one more time.

"What is your secret?

Robert laughed, "You will find out tomorrow lass, just wait and see."

Annie said okay. She did not really care right now. Her Robert was home and she was happy just to be in his strong arms again. They fell asleep and Annie dreamed of Rita standing in the woods and the life of so long ago.

Annie woke first and went down stairs to get breakfast. Just as she was going to call Robert, Joey appeared at the top of the stairs.

"Is Daddy home?"

"Yes, your father is home, but he is still in bed." Annie said. Joey didn't hear the last words he was running down the hall to Robert's room and jumped on the bed.

"Daddy what did you bring me?" he asked just bubbling over with excitement. "Shhhh, wait until the wagon gets here and you shall see."

Robert and Joey soon came down for breakfast and as they were eating Annie asked, "Well, how did the trip go? Was the castle in ruins?"

"The castle is in need of a lot of repairs and it will take some time to complete them but I have men working on it now."

"Did it take so long just to check the castle out?" Annie asked.

"Well no," Robert answered sheepishly, "I went some where to pick up a few things that were needed, and that is all I have to say."

There was a knock on the door and Annie walked over and opened it. One of Robert's men stood there and asked, "Can I see Robert?"

Annie turned, "There is some one to see you." she said to Robert.

Robert and the man went into the main room talking in hushed tones. After several minutes, Robert returned. Smiling at Annie, he said, "I will be right back." and walked outside with the man following him.

Annie was more then a little puzzled. She served Joey breakfast and sat down to eat something herself. The door opened again and Robert and the man walked in carrying rather large bags. Annie looked at Robert as the men walked over to the utility table and laid the bags down.

"Well, don't just sit there, open your presents."

Annie slowly walked over, not knowing what to expect. Gingerly, she untied one of the large bags. She gasped as the aroma drifted upwards. She looked in the bag, reached in and pulled out a bag of coffee beans. After all these years wanting a good cup of coffee, she was going to have one. Tears rolled down her cheeks as she recalled how easy it used to be, going to the supermarket and buying whatever she wanted. People just don't know how easy they have it, until they lose what they have. She turned and gave Robert a big hug. This was the most wonderful thing she could have hoped for.

"Are you going to open the other bag mommy?" Joey asked.

Annie turned to the other bag, but Joey was already untying the cord. He stepped back. "What is this stuff/" he said.

Annie looked and it was of all things, sugar, pure white sugar. Annie threw her arms around again. "Robert! Oh! Where did you get all this?" she cried.

"Do I get any presents?" Joey shouted.

"I will tell you all about it later." Robert said with a wink to Annie. Turning to Joey, Robert said "Go and look in the wagon and tell me if you like them."

Joey ran outside. They could hear him shout with joy. Joey came back holding a beautiful pair of handmade leather riding boots. Joey took great pains putting the boots on and walked all around the room. Going over to Robert, he was picked up bodily and twirled in a circle. He put his little arms around his neck.

"Oh thank you daddy! I have always wanted some just like this."

Robert turned to Annie, "Well? Do I get a cup of this stuff called coffee?" Annie rushed off to the kitchen and after much thought came up with a crude way of crushing the beans and cooking them. Before long she had a pot of steaming coffee. After pouring it into mugs, she put the precious sugar in and a splash of cream. Setting it in front of Robert she smiled.

"Be careful. It is hot."

He took a careful sip, then another. "So this is coffee." He paused thoughtfully, "It does taste good. It is very good, I think, since I have never tasted it before. I have never tasted anything like this."

After they finished the coffee Robert got up and said, "Oh! Lass, I have other things for you. I am sure Joey found the rest of the things I got for him."

Robert went out the wagon and after a few minutes Annie followed. Just as she got to the wagon, Joey jumped out with a huge mask that Robert brought from Africa. Robert walked to the other side of the wagon and pulled the tarp off. Annie saw bag after bag of spices and cloth he had gotten for her and Lilly.

"Oh Robert! This is just too wonderful." she said as she threw her arms around him again. They returned to the house, leaving Lilly and Angus to unload and store the rest of the newly acquired bounty. When they were alone, Annie questioned Robert about the rampant rumors that were circulating. The word was that there was a band of cutthroats running loose. Did he know anything?

"Lass, I want you and Joey to stay close to the house because word is James the Terrible is on the rampage again."

Chapter 15

Rita drove back to the hotel, deep in thought. Maybe she should think about buying a small house. There are so many unanswered questions. The more information she acquires the more she seems to need. "I don't think I will be going back to the states anytime soon." She said out loud.

She stopped at the local real estate office and put in her request for a small cottage. The gentleman at the office told her there was one not too far out of town but it needed fixing up. Rita agreed to drive out after lunch. She went into the little pub down the street. She took much longer than anticipated and when she arrived back at the real- estate office the man was pacing in front of the office. The drive was quiet lovely with all the trees and mountains in the distance. After about a thirty-minute drive they pulled up a long circular drive and Rita saw the most beautiful old cottage she had ever seen. Much to the man's surprise Rita announced she would take it before they had even gotten out of the car. Rita sat transfixed, staring at the house. The outside of the cottage was covered with vines to such an extent it was almost impossible to see what it was made of. There was a spot or two were some old stone work was visible. A window to the left was broken. Off to the right of the front door was a large picture window with many small panes of glass.

"Wait." the man said. "Look at the whole place before you commit to such a venture as this."

They stepped out of the car. The man walked to the front door, pulling a set of keys from his pocket, and unlocked the front door. Rita walked into the cottage. The light, which came through the open door and broken window, revealed a kitchen area. A table was standing on its own with two chairs, one broken and the other on its side. There was a fireplace off to the left. The air was stale and musty indicating that the house hadn't been opened for a long time. The man followed her into the house, turning on a flashlight, which he had taken from his other pocket. Shining it around the kitchen, it fell on the frightened face of a squirrel that jumped from the fireplace to the table and out the broken window.

"As you can see, it is not in very good condition. It has been vacant for a long time. I believe it was originally built two hundred years ago. There are many things needing repair. All the floors are still good but the roof is in very bad shape and should be replaced as quickly as possible. I am not sure it is repairable. The grounds just need a little bit of attention to get rid of the overgrowth. If you have a green thumb, you could plant new flowers." He added optimistically. He couldn't help noticing a look of awe on Rita's face. She was indeed taken by the old cottage. He continued, "Someone from town can fix the old stones, on the outside of the house, that needs replacing. We have several good stone masons in the area. The stones came from a quarry not far from here. Would you like to look through the rest of the cottage?"

"Yes I would."

Suddenly concerned about the young lady's capabilities, the man scratched his head and said, "This is a lot for someone like you to handle."

"What do you mean?" Rita asked.

"Well, it will take a considerable amount of money just to make it livable.

Please don't take this the wrong way, but you are a young woman and may not realize what you are getting into."

"Money is not a problem. And as for my abilities, my father was a carpenter, and I am not without some knowledge of what needs to be done. Can I see the rest of the house?"

"Yes Ma'am." Was the reply and he led her through it with the flashlight. There were two small rooms, which could be bedrooms, and one bathroom that contained an old claw footed tub and rust covered sink. The sink would need to be replaced, but the beautiful antique tub was definitely salvageable. They walked through a large front room, which connected back to the kitchen. There was the picture window she had seen from the outside. It gave a view of the overgrown front yard.

Upon their return to the kitchen, Rita asked, "When can we get started with the paperwork?"

"If you are really sure about this, I can start it today, and have things ready for your signature tomorrow afternoon. Will that be alright for you?" he inquired.

"I definitely want it. Tomorrow will be fine." Rita was elated. They rode back to office in relative silence. Rita kept imagining the cottage in her mind. How would she make repairs? What would have to be done by others? Decorating? Yard work? When they arrived back at his office, Rita wrote out a check and gave it to the realtor.

"This should be sufficient for now to show I am serious. Just let me know if you need more to get repairs started. If you need me, I can be reached at the hotel down the street." The man acknowledged her, looked at the check, and thanked her again. Rita went back to the hotel with thoughts whirling around in her head. When she got to her room, she ran a tub of water and poured some bubble bath in it. Rita lay in the warm bubbly water very pleased and smug with herself with all she had accomplished. After drying her hair and slipping into her nightgown she fell into the large bed utterly exhausted.

She woke the next morning rested and laid there thinking of all the things that to look forward to in the weeks ahead. Rita went down stairs and ordered breakfast thinking about the kind of furniture she wanted. She wanted everything to fit the period of the house. She would have to find someone to help her with that. After breakfast she went back to the real estate office where she found the man on the phone lining up contracts to start work that day. The man motioned for Rita to sit down which she did. She was glad she he was handling everything because he was so exact and sure of himself on the phone giving orders and telling someone what was to be done. Ten minutes later he put down the phone and smiled at Rita.

"Well, the work is underway. What can I help you with today?

"I need to know where I can find an interior decorator to furnish the house."

The man flipped through an old Rolodex on his desk. "Here is just the woman you need, Miss McGruder. She has done a lot of work over the years for us and knows all about the type of things you are probably interested in."

With address in hand, Rita set off for the furniture store in town. Rita found the woman in a small office in the back of the store. The office was piled high with scores of books which impressed Rita with the idea the woman was a person deeply involved with her work. She was in her sixties and very petite with a bun on the top of her head. The suit she had on looked like it came from the twenties but when she spoke Rita took an instant liking to her. She had a way of putting one at ease and was very knowledgeable of Scottish history and furnishings of two hundred years ago. The two women sat for what seemed like just a few minutes, but when Rita got up to leave she saw it was twelve o'clock. The time had flown and Miss McGruder, or Kathy as she said she would rather be referred to, had everything under control. They had picked out the furniture, drapes and the most gorgeous throw rugs. All Rita had to do now was sit back and let everyone handle things. Rita went to the hotel, had a sandwich and went to her room. She was worn out so she laid down for a nap.

The phone jarred her out of a sound sleep, grabbing the phone she heard a voice. "Rita? Are you there?"

"Who is this?" Rita was half asleep and the voice seemed far away. "This is Hanna, you need to come out to my house now. Something has happened that you need to see." Rita glanced at the clock. It was four o'clock. My God! I must have been awful tired to sleep almost four hours. Hanna sounded very excited.

"Okay. I'll be there as soon as possible." Rita got up, brushed her hair, splashed water on her face, went down stairs, got in her car and took off. Rita was at Hanna's house in record time. She was sitting on the front steps of her cottage when Rita drove up. Before Rita could stop her car, the old woman was up and on her way to greet her.

"Oh! Rita! You have to see this!" Hanna took her hand as she got out of the car and led her to the woods behind her house. As they got closer Rita saw a huge black horse just standing there. "Wait! That is not all!" she exclaimed.

Rita heard a muffled sound and then a small boy appeared from behind the massive horse. He was crying and holding his left arm. Rita slowly walked toward the boy and his horse, the child was clean and well nourished. His hair was a little long and mussed but his eyes were clear and had a touch of defiance in them. The big horse eyed her suspiciously and snorted loudly as she approached. His hoof pawed the ground. Rita did not want to spook the horse or the child so she stopped several feet away and squatted down.

"Hi honey." she said. "What is your name?

The child lowered his head. "I am not allowed to talk to people I do not know." he said with a deep Scottish brogue.

"My name is Rita." she said. "What is your name?

The little boy sniffled, kicked at the dirt and very softly whispered, "Joey. I. I fell off my daddy's horse and hurt my arm real bad." With tears rolling down his face he continued, "I am not allowed to ride him and I am in a lot of trouble." Rita was reeling. "My God!" she thought, "Could this be Annie's Joey?" Rita stood up and walked a couple of steps closer but stopped when the horse made a menacing move. Rita spoke very low. "Is your horse named Max?" The boy looked at her suspiciously and answered slowly, "He is not my horse. My arm hurts, bad!" He kept looking at the lady, not sure if she could be trusted. How did she know Max? He had never seen her before.

Rita felt her face drain and almost fainted. "Is your mommy named Annie?" she asked.

Again the boy looked at her with apparent surprise on his face. "And your daddy's name is Robert, isn't it?" she continued.

'Sir Robert!" Joey said indignantly, "and how do you know? I have never seen you before? I don't know you." he said defiantly as he wiped the tears from his face.

Rita turned and looked at Hanna. Instead of seeing the shock she expected, Rita saw her smiling at the young lad. Rita turned back to the boy. "Would you let me look at your arm?"

"No, it hurts. When I fell I heard a noise." he said.

Rita was having a hard time breathing. She had never been so excited. "I promise not to hurt you." she told the apprehensive Joey.

"Are you sure? he asked.

Rita took another step closer to them. "Yes. I promise." Rita noticed the huge horse's eyes get wide with fear. He stepped back a step and seemed braced for battle. "Easy Max, its okay big boy. I won't hurt him." Her voice was calm but her heart was pounding as she started to approach them.

Joey backed up a step too. He wanted help but he still was not sure this stranger could be trusted. Rita stopped again as Joey spoke, "How do you know his name? And my mommy and daddy? Why don't I know you?" Joey asked with his head cocked sideways.

"We can talk about that later. Right now I think I should look at your arm."

Joey turned and looked up at Max. He placed his good hand up in front of the horse's face and said, "Stay." Max shook his head and snorted as if to say "No way!" "Stay!" Joey repeated and the horse stood still. Hesitantly Joey walked towards Rita.

"Come on, I won't bite you." She smiled at him. Then all of a sudden he was there in front of her. She reached out to touch him. She very carefully ran her fingers down his arm.

"Ouch!" tears started to come to his eyes again. Rita felt the bone in his forearm. Yes, it is broken. Rita turned to Hanna.

"I can't take him to the hospital. What can I do?"

Without hesitation Hanna said "Well, can't you mend it here?"

"It is a simple fracture," Rita agreed, "could you go to the pharmacy in town and get a few things for me?"

"What do you need?" Hanna asked.

"I need some one-inch gauze and plaster of Paris and a large bottle of non- aspirin." Hanna didn't hesitate. Rita told her the car keys were in her purse and Hanna was off to the drug store. Rita sat down by the boy.

"Why are you dressed so funny?" Joey asked, "And how do you know my mommy and daddy?"

Chapter 16

Annie was thrilled to have all the spices and material Robert had gotten. Now she could make curtains for all the rooms. Annie stopped and looked around "Where is Joey?" she asked Robert.

"Oh, he wanted to show Max his new things. I told him he could play out in the trees until we finished."

Annie continued to oversee the unloading and then went into the house. Lilly was giving orders and enjoying every minute. Lilly walked around the kitchen, shaking her head is dismay. "I will have to have more storage space for all the things that man brought back." She said in an irritated way.

But Annie knew Lilly was thrilled to have things to help with her cooking. Annie went back out to the garden to get a few things for the special dinner she wanted to cook that night. After getting the vegetables she wanted, she went back inside to find Lilly still busy putting things away. "I will cook dinner tonight." Annie told her.

Without turning Lilly said, "Good, because I may be up all night finding a place for everything."

Annie laughed and started dinner. Dinner was almost ready and it was time to set the table before Annie wondered where Joey was. She went to the door and called Robert. "Find Joey and come in for dinner." she told him. Robert went off to find Joey and Annie sat down on the steps to wait. When Robert came back he went straight to the stable. This made Annie nervous and she headed to the stable also. She found Robert talking to Angus in a breathless way. He turned and seeing Annie said, "Not to worry, Lass. Joey just took Max off. He will be safe with him but we are going out to find them." Angus had finished saddling two horses. He and Robert mounted them and went off towards the woods again, calling Joey's name. Annie started to worry; it was not like Joey to stray far from the house. Annie went off in the other direction on the other side of the great house to look for him.

Chapter 17

Hanna got back with the things from the pharmacy and Rita told her to go and get some water for the plaster of paris, a pen and paper. Hanna got the water and Rita set about soaking the plaster. Then she wrapped the gauge around Joey's arm. When the plaster had softened she carefully wrapped it around the gauge, Joey sat wide eyed the whole time not saying a word. Rita finished and rubbed the plaster smooth.

"There, you are all set and ready to go home." She quickly wrote a note to Annie and slipped it into Joey's pocket. "Now go home and tell your mommy that Aunt Rita fixed your arm. She will know what to do after that." As Joey got up, Rita added, "Oh! Tell your mommy it was not near the growth plate. She will understand. Can, you remember to say that?"

"Yes. I will say just what you said." Joey answered as he stared at the hardening cast.

Rita walked Joey to the edge of the woods. He turned to her again with a look of confusion and asked, "How do you now my mommy and daddy?"

"Oh I knew them a very long time ago." Rita told him and that seemed to satisfy him. Rita reached up and stroked Max on the nose. "Take care of my little friend." Then she bent down and gave Joey a big hug.

Hanna ran up to them, holding something out in front of her, "You forgot the pills."

"Oh yes. Thank you." Rita gave them to Joey. "Give these to your mommy; she will know what they are for." Rita and Hanna stood and watched Joey walk several yards into the woods with Max at his side. He turned and waved once, then took a few more steps and disappeared.

Rita blinked, and then just stood there for what seemed like forever. "I still can't believe this is really happening." She said to no one, for when she turned around she realized Hanna had gone back to her home.

Rita went back to Hanna's house where she found her in the kitchen brewing tea. Rita took the cups out of the cupboard and sat them on the table. Hanna poured the tea, sat down and said, "Okay, tell me what just happened. A kid, obviously from not around here, not of this time, and you act like you have known him for years."

"Let's go out on the porch and I will try and explain everything to you."

Quite awhile later, Rita finished and Hanna sat quietly. "Well now I have heard everything. So that is why you came to Scotland, to try and reach your friend."

"No, I had no idea anything like this would happen. I just wanted to try and be close to where Annie lived. Do you think I am crazy to have thoughts like that?" she asked Hanna.

"No, I think you were blessed to have had the encounter with the wee lad."

"I do feel very lucky. It was almost like seeing Annie again. Well, I do have to run. It is getting late. May I come back I want you to see the house I bought."

"You are welcome anytime." Hanna said. As Rita was walking she heard Hanna laugh Rita turned and asked what was so funny. "What will those people think about the cast on that child's arm?"

Rita stopped and started laughing also. "Yes, that will be a Kodak moment." Rita laughed as she got in her car and drove to the hotel. Upon her arrival she found several messages from the real estate agent. The desk clerk told Rita she was to call a Mr. Andrews at home and gave her the number. Rita was starving but went to her room and called him. He sounded very upset when she reached him. He went on to explain that there was going to be a delay getting the stones from the quarry. Rita did not understand why he was so upset and told him not to worry. It was okay. He sounded very relieved and told Rita he would stay in touch. Evidently he was concerned that if he didn't provide everything on time, she would pull out of the transaction and he would lose a rather large commission. Rita did not feel like going back down stairs, so she called room service and ordered a large steak and salad.

Chapter 18

Annie was getting frantic. She had gone fairly deep into the forest behind the house calling Joey's name. Convincing herself he would not have come this far with Max, she turned and headed back. She walked past the great house and towards the trees and trails that Robert and Angus had gone to. Max appeared suddenly at the edge of the forest, and Joey was standing beside him. Annie began to run toward them. As she approached she sensed different or abnormal with Joey. He stood funny or was holding something or... She stopped short and threw her hands to her face to stifle a scream. Joey's arm was wrapped up in what looked like a...cast? Annie began to run again to Joey. He just stood still and waited for her, not sure if he was in trouble for taking Max, or getting hurt or talking to strangers, or what. When Annie reached him his tears began again, but Annie was staring instead at the cast on his arm.

"Mommy, I fell off Max and I hurt my arm and something strange happened and two ladies where there and she knows you and fixed my arm and I was scared and I'm sorry and....and..." the rest of his story was muffled as Annie fell to hers knees and held him close to her. After several seconds she leaned back and looked at him.

"It's okay, Joey. It's okay. Stop crying, you will be alright You are not in any trouble. We were just worried about you. Now tell me what happened to you. Slowly, please."

"Well when I was in the woods riding Max, something scared him and I fell. There was a lady, two ladies, who were dressed funny. One knew my name, and yours and daddy's and Max. But I don't know her, who was she Mommy? The other lady, she was older, just stood there. I was scared but she said she knew all of us. My arm hurt and she made it feel better. Look," he said as he tapped it with his knuckle, "it's hard, like a stone."

There was the sound of approaching horses. Robert and Angus reined in. Robert jumped down and looked at Joey. "What's that?" He said as he pointed at Joey's arm.

"Robert, you and Angus take the horses to the barn. I will take Joey in the house and check out his arm. Come in the house when you are done and I will tell you what you need to know."

Robert took the reins of Max and started for the barn with Angus. In the house Annie sat Joey down at the table. "You sit and I will fix something for you. Now go ahead and tell me what happened."

"I was riding Max and something scared him. He reared up and I fell off. I heard something crack in my arm. I was just standing there, crying, not knowing what to do when I heard a voice and saw the lady. She seemed very nice, but Max would not let her come close to me. Not until she spoke to him and used his name. She looked at my arm and told me it was broken. She was really nice and knew all of us. Mommy, how come she knows us and I don't know her. How is that, mommy?" he asked. "I have never seen her. And she talked funny and was dressed funny. She had pants on and she smelled pretty. She said the break was not near my plate or something like that."

"Your growth plate." Annie interrupted, as she set a cup of milk and some buttered bread before him.

Robert entered the kitchen and walked straight to Joey. He reached out and touched his cast. "An what is this thing the boy has on his arm? An where did it come from? An why did you take Max out in the first place?" he asked with as much anger as he could muster considering how worried he was.

'Sit down and let him finish his story." Annie told Robert as she poured him a cup of coffee. Robert and Joey looked at her strangely. "Go on and finish."

"The nice lady stayed with me and Max. She sent the other lady away to get some, ah, stuff. I tried to ask her questions and tell her I had to go home, but my arm hurt and she said she could fix it. When the other lady came back, she wrapped some funny looking soft white cloth around my arm and then some wet white stuff. She gave me this." Joey took the large bottle of children's pills from his pocket and handed them to Annie who took the bottle of pills and smiled. "Oh, and she gave me this too," pulling the note out of his pocket.

Annie opened the note, read a little and gasped. "Oh my God, I don't believe…" she looked back at the note.

"My Dear Annie, I put your wonderful gift to good use. I am now a physician. I don't know if I will go back to the states or stay here. This is such a beautiful place, and I have bought a lovely old cottage I am having restored. I gave a rather large amount of the money to the children's floor for a playroom with all the latest games for the kids. There is a gold plaque with the words "Joey's Room" *on the door. Your Joey is a doll and a very brave boy, you've done a great job. I really can't believe this is happening, but it must be. I will find a way to stay in touch. Love, Rita "*

After reading it twice, she just sat there staring at Robert. "Rita is a Doctor. She made it. She really did. She went through school and became a physician and she thanked me for the money I left her." Annie read it again and a tear fell on her cheek "Rita said Joey is very brave."

"Is that all she said?"

"No, she bought a cottage and is going to live in Scotland. Oh Robert," she threw her arms around his neck, "I feel so close to her." Coming back to reality, she bent down to look at Joey's arm. "Does your arm still hurt honey?"

"No, not too much." he said, "The lady gave me something funny tasting and it stopped. Who is Miss Rita, Mommy?"

"I guess you could say she is your guardian angel. That is the second time in your life she has helped you." she said.

Joey cocked his head and looked very puzzled. "I'm not sure I understand. You are acting funny."

"Yes honey, I know." Annie said laughing, "but its okay. Don't worry yourself about it. It will take some time. You will understand better when you are older."

"Mommy can I go and show John my new cast tomorrow? When his daddy broke his hand and you just wrapped it up. But this is different."

Annie looked at Robert, then back at Joey. "We will talk about that tomorrow okay? Now you go get ready for supper."

Annie was very concerned about Joey and the questions he was bound to ask. How would she answer them? Supper was an ordeal for

Annie. She could sense the questions that Joey had but was unable to express. Robert also seemed to be unusually quiet. After supper Annie took Joey up to bed. She carefully removed his shirt, being as gentle as she could. She sponged him off, helped him with his nightshirt and gave him another pill. He said his prayers, including a special thank you for his "guardian angel," and was tucked in by Annie.

"You sleep tight, honey. I'll check in on you later. You may have some trouble getting comfortable but it will be okay. If you wake up and your arm is hurting, you come and get me. Okay? I know you had a strange day, but I promise everything will be alright."

"Okay Mommy." Annie kissed him goodnight, blew out the candle and left the room. She returned to the kitchen and sat down with Robert.

"Lass," Robert said, "I think it is high time to talk about Joey getting his education."

Annie looked at him, "What do you mean? I teach him every day."

"No, Lass. I mean it is time we sent him away to learn things that boys need to know. Things you nor I can teach him. He will find out how to work with other boys. The dangers they face in this world and all the other things they need to know to stay alive. He will learn to be a man someday."

Annie knew in her head he was right but her heart screamed "No." "Why can't we give him another year or so?" Annie pleaded. Robert was a very levelheaded and stubborn man, but sometimes Annie could twist him around her finger.

"Well would you settle on going to England for a while instead?" he asked. "Yes, I think that would be fun. Joey has never been away from home and I think he would enjoy that. Of course, we will have to wait until his arm has healed. I don't think it would be wise to around the countryside with that cast on it…" Annie said with a chuckle.

"Robert laughed with her, stood, stretched and winked, "I agree. But right now I am ready for bed, how about you?"

Smiling, she took his hand and they went up the stairs to bed. While Annie's mind was on the moment at hand, she couldn't help thinking that somehow she would find a way to wait until Joey was older, much older, before she would allow him to go traipsing off to another country to "become a man" as Robert had put it.

Chapter 19

Rita woke up rather late and lay in bed thinking of everything she wanted to do that day. She needed to shop for clothes because she would be staying much longer then originally planned. Rita got out of bed, dressed, and grabbed a cup of Cappuccino at the coffee shop next door to the hotel, and set out on her shopping spree. She was glad to see there were a number of shops she could choose from within walking distance of the hotel. After leaving instructions to have everything sent to her hotel, she went to see the interior decorator to finalize furniture and materials. Walking out of the store in a bit of a hurry, she collided with the most handsome man she had ever seen. Embarrassed, she excused herself quickly and stared momentarily at his exquisite features.

"Oh, no! It is I who should be sorry. Are you okay?" he asked in a beautiful Scottish accent.

"Yes. I'm fine."

"Well I am truly sorry for bumping into you. Please let me buy you a cup of tea." he said motioning to a little restaurant next to the interior decorators. "Please say yes. I won't hurt you. I promise." he smiled at her.

Realizing she hadn't eaten anything for several hours, and considering the handsome gentleman's sincerity, Rita responded, "Tea would be fine."

They found a table in the small restaurant and sat down. After ordering the tea he introduced himself, "My name is William McClancy." extending his hand to her.

Accepting his handshake Rita said, "Rita Richards." "Are you here on a holiday?" he asked.

Rita thought quickly. She could not tell this stranger that she was here to find out about her dead friend. "Well I have just put in six grueling years in med school and residency and felt like I needed a rather long vacation. I have no idea how long I may be here. It could be a few months or a couple of years. I don't know really."

"Well that is nice. We need good doctors here. It would be good if you stayed." "Who knows," Rita said nonchalantly. "I just might do that. But I can not make up my mind at this time. What do you do?" She asked wanting to get the subject off of herself.

"I have that little sports car dealership down the street. It belonged to my father until he died last year. Then I took it over. Come on over and I will put you in a sharp little two seater." he said.

Rita laughed. "Well I'm looking at a cottage right now and I have a lot of work ahead of me if I go ahead with it. Maybe after that I will pay you a visit." Rita still wasn't too sure of this handsome salesman and was not about to tell him everything.

"I hope you don't wait too long to come and see me. That would be a disappointment." William paused to see if Rita would respond. She on the other hand also knew how to play the game and just smiled at him. So William bowed his head with old fashioned courtesy and said, "Well madam, I am at your disposal if needed. I do have to get back to the office." He raised his eyebrows as if to be thinking and then continued, "But I don't work all the time. Would you care to have dinner with me tonight?"

Rita only had to think about that for a second. "That would be very nice. I am still learning my way around. I am staying at *The Kings Inn*."

"Would seven be alright?" he asked. "That would be fine."

"Well I will see you then." Again he bowed, turned and walked off.

Rita just stood there for a moment looking after him. Then she turned and began to return to her hotel. She walked with a smile on her face and in her heart. I am so glad I went shopping today she thought to herself.

Rita went to her room and found she had a message from Hanna. She called her and they had a long talk. Rita told her she would be out there in a couple of days for a visit. Rita looked at her watch and went to run a tub of water. She wanted to get to a phone store to get new cell phone. That was one convenience she had missed while driving around. The bath did her a world of good. She loved the new dress and shoes she had purchased earlier. She had enough time to get to the phone store, get a new cell phone and have it activated. Then she headed back to the hotel to meet William for dinner. As she neared the hotel she saw he was out front about to enter.

"Hello." She called to him. He turned toward her and waved. Her breath caught in her throat, he was so good looking. He was tall with sandy hair and had on the most elegant looking suit. He just oozed masculinity.

"Sorry I'm late." She said as she reached him.

"No. No, not at all. I am early. I was just anxious to see you again. I hope I didn't interrupt your schedule." Rita shook her head no. "The restaurant is just around the corner. I have my car here or would you rather walk?"

"It's a lovely evening, let's walk."

They proceeded down the cobble stoned street. Rita couldn't help notice once again the quaintness of the area. All the shops were so small and close, nothing like the vast malls of the U. S. They came to the restaurant and went inside. The maitre d' knew William and greeted them cordially. Rita felt like royalty as he escorted them to a quiet table away from the entrance and kitchen. It was partially secluded by plant boxes filled with beautiful ivy and potted trees. He left them with a menu and wine list. After they ordered and the drinks arrived William asked why Rita chose Scotland to live. Rather than tell him the real reason, she told him that her ancestors had come from there and she wanted to see what Scotland was like. When she arrived she fell in love with it, which was not he whole truth but it served the purpose for now. She still did not know William well enough to tell him about all the strange occurrences that she has endured of late.

The dinner was fabulous, with good food and excellent service. He told her all about his life and his travels. He graduated from *Eaton University*. Rita could have listened to his stories all night long. His accent sounded like music to her. Just as she was thinking how she did not want the night to end, William broke into her reverie, "Well, I must get up early." He said. "I don't want to, but I think I should take you back to the hotel."

Rita looked at her watch. It was eleven thirty. "Oh!" she said, "where has the time gone? This has been such a wonderful evening. I have to get out to the cottage early in the morning also. The interior decorator is going to be there to give me some of her ideas."

They walked hand in hand down the street to Rita's hotel and when they were in front of the hotel they just stood awkwardly at first. "Rita, I have had one of the most enjoyable evenings that I can remember. Thank you for the pleasure of your company."

"Thank you William. It has been a wonderful evening for me also." She smiled up at him. He leaned over and kissed her tenderly.

"May I call on you again? Maybe you will let me take you out and acquaint you with some of our beautiful countryside."

"I think that would be just fine."

"Well, good night. I'll call you as soon as I can."

Rita went to the elevator. She could only think how very different William was from all the other men she had dated in the past. He was a real gentleman and that was what she had been waiting for all these years. Rita got to her room and changed into her nightgown and lay down but for some reason was not the least bit sleepy. She reached over grabbed the television remote and tuned in some old movie, the next thing she knew the phone was ringing. It was Mrs. McRuder, the interior decorator. Rita looked at the clock and it was ten thirty. She had promised to meet her at nine. Rita apologized, dressed in a hurry and rushed over to the store.

Mrs. McRuder laughed and told Rita there was no big rush. It wasn't necessary for her to hurry over like that. Rita felt differently, she wanted to have her own home where she could freedom and privacy. The two women looked at material and glass wear all morning Rita realized it was past lunch and she hadn't eaten anything.

"I'm starving. Let's go get some lunch. It's on me." She said. Rita and Mrs. McRuder went down to the little pub and enjoyed the good food. They discussed the final decisions about everything in the cottage. Rita felt good about it. She had picked out the material for the chairs, couch and the drapes. She felt like things were going along quite well. If everything else goes as smoothly as today, then she should have her home ready for company before too long. William crossed her mind and Rita smiled at the idea of company. She was very pleased indeed.

Chapter 20

Annie slipped out of bed and went over to the window. She was having trouble sleeping due to all the things that had happened the day before. They made her very uneasy. She stood at the window and gazed out into the night sky. There was a full moon. She could see a doe and her fawn nibbling on the damp grass at the edge of the forest. All of a sudden they bolted and disappeared into the forest, frightened by something. Standing very still, Annie looked carefully to see what it might have been. The night sky had a strange orange glow to it. Annie thought she smelled something funny. She opened the window, placed her hands on the sill and leaned out. There was something in the air, a smell, and it was stronger now. Looking out over the trees the orange glow was brighter and she was hearing something else, strange sounds. Suddenly her blood ran cold. The glow was from a fire, the village was burning. The sounds were those of the people screaming and the crackling of the fire itself.

"Robert!" she called as she turned from the window. He had already sensed a problem or her absence from their bed. In any case Robert was out of bed and almost had his pants on when Annie turned to him. He ran over to the window. By now flames could be seen above the treetops.

"Lass, go get the boy and Lilly and go to the root cellar." Annie stood there, eyes full of fright. "Go! Now! There is no time for talk." he commanded.

Annie went to Joey's room. He was sitting up in bed. "What is all the noise?" he asked sleepily. Keeping her voice as calm as she could, Annie threw some clothes on the bed and told him to dress quickly.

"Then come to the kitchen. We have to go to the root cellar. No questions. Hurry."

Then she ran downstairs and woke up Lilly. They were in the kitchen putting some water and bread in a basket when Joey came in.

"Where is daddy? What is the matter?" Joey cried.

"Daddy will be with us soon. There is a fire in the village and we have to go to the root cellar. Take this basket and come with us, everything will be okay. Just hurry." As they went out into the hall, Robert was going out the front door.

"I will come get you when things are safe. Angus and I will go to town to help." he shouted.

Joey held tight to Annie's skirt with one hand and clutched the small basket of bread with the other. "Are we going to die?"

"No Honey, of course not. We just need to stay where it will be safe. We will be fine."

As they were going to the back of the house, where the entrance was, Annie could see Robert talking to Angus. They ran into the barn. Annie helped Lilly get Joey into the root cellar, and then started down herself. She paused and turned back to look toward the village. The flames were leaping high into the night sky and she could hear people yelling and screaming. Annie took a candle from her pocket, lit it and passed it to Lillie. She slammed the door closed and huddled close to Joey and Lilly. Even with the flickering candlelight, it was still dark and damp. The root cellar was several feet below ground level, about five feet wide and ten feet long. They were sitting on benches hewn from the nearby forest. Annie worried about what else might be was down in the dank musty cellar. She heard hoofs thundering across the ground above. She knew Robert and Angus were going to get Robert's men to help fight the fire. But would they have enough time to gather them and return before the village was destroyed. Annie sat quietly talking to Joey reassuring him that things would be okay.

It was some time later, maybe thirty minutes or so, when the cellar door shook and dust fell all around them. An unknown number of horses had galloped by. After waiting several seconds, Annie slipped over to the door and opened it cautiously, enough to see Robert and about thirty or so men riding towards the village. She was happy the men were there but was concerned for their safety. The sun was beginning to rise in the east and a layer of smoke hung in the air. Annie closed the cellar door. All they could do now was to wait for Robert to return safely and give them the all clear to come out. Lilly sang a Scottish lullaby to Joey to keep his mind off what was happening outside. There was a strong smell of smoke drifting down into the cellar. Hot cinders fell from above. The manor must be on fire. What were they going to do? They were trapped. Several minutes went by. Just when Annie was going to look outside again, the cellar door was suddenly flung open. Annie saw a ragged dirty man with wet and dried blood running down the side of his face peer down at them. She screamed.

Lilly touched Annie's arm. "It's Master Robert." she whispered. Joey jumped ahead of them, "Daddy! Daddy!" he yelled.

Annie reached out and stopped him.

"We have to get Daddy in here." she told him. Confused, Joey turned and looked at Annie. Robert came into the cellar and sat on the steps. The door remained open behind him. He had a few burns and cuts, but he was fine. She thought he looked a lot worse then he was.

It is okay. Why did you scream? That was a fine thing to do, Lass. Did I scare you that badly?" Annie could not find her voice. All she could do was look at Robert in the dimly lit root cellar. The combination of semi dark from within and early daylight cast weird shadows on his face. Her feelings were total relief that he was alive and horror at his condition. When Annie was able to speak, she asked if everything was destroyed.

"Well the manor will need some work but for the most part, it stood up quiet well. Only the east wing was destroyed by the fire." Annie could see out the open cellar door and could see the men running toward the barn. Robert and Annie stepped out of the cellar and looked at the still smoldering fire but everything did look in fairly good shape. She looked towards the manor and with the sun rising could see the damage done. Annie laid her head on Robert's shoulder in relief when a gasp came from Robert and he slumped to the ground. Annie screamed. She saw a broken arrow shaft sticking out from his shoulder. Several men came over and helped put Robert on a litter. He was still alive but in a great deal of pain. The kitchen area of the house was still sound so Annie had the men take him in and place the litter on the table.

"Lilly, put some water on to boil, I'm going to look at this wound."

Chapter 21

Rita was still very pleased and excited about all that she had accomplished. After lunch she returned to the interior decorators and went back over their choices one more time. It was mid afternoon when she left Mrs. McRuder and went back to the hotel. Just as she was undressing the phone rang. Somehow she knew it was William and it was. He was asking her out. He told her he wanted to try out a new sports car and would she like to go for a drive in the country. Needless to say her answer was yes. She took a bath and dressed and went downstairs just about the time he drove up. William bounced out of the car and opened the door for her and soon they were speeding along a lovely country road, everything was so peaceful Rita wanted it to stay that way forever. They stopped a country inn and had a wonderful supper then went for a walk in the small village.

"Oh look," Rita announced, "There is an old antique store. Let's go in and see if they have anything for my house."

They went in and it was like a whole different world. The old man behind the counter was bent over with arthritis and could barely walk, but was very friendly and most helpful. Rita found several things that would go perfect in the front room of the cottage and an old iron pot that she wanted to place in the yard. As the old man added things up William reached for his wallet. Rita tried to stop him.

"It's just a house warming gift. You cannot say no to that. Someday you can repay me by cooking dinner for me."

"Ok." Rita smiled and allowed him to pay for the few things and then they were on their way. Rita was not used to this much open space and enjoyed it. "Is this what it is going to be like living here?" she said aloud.

William smiled and said he hoped she would like living here because he did not plan on her ever leaving. William stopped in another village in front of a quaint little house.

"This is where I was born and grew up." he said. Rita did not know too much about him and asked about family. "Well my mother became very sick after I was born and could not have more children. She died when I was five and my father raised me. He never remarried. My mother was his only love."

"What happened to your father?"

"He died of a heart attack two years ago."

"Oh, I'm sorry." Rita sensed sadness in his voice and decided to stop talking for now. Besides she was not ready to tell William about her family so she just sat back and enjoyed the ride. The night was beautifully clear and the stars all shined brightly.

Back at the Inn, William ended it with a promise of more surprises tomorrow. They said good night and Rita went to her room. She watched a little news then turned in for the night. Her sleep was not restful; she had a very disturbing night full of nightmares. Thankfully, when she woke she could not remember them.

As she was sitting down for breakfast her cell phone rang and it was Hanna. She sounded very upset and asked Rita to please come out to her house quickly. Rita finished her coffee and went to her car thinking "What could be the problem this time?" Rita drove to her house as fast as she could. As she pulled up in front Hanna was standing outside looking rather frantic. Rita rushed over.

"What is wrong?"

"Come. Out back. By the woods." Hanna spoke in choppy sentences and motioned for Rita to follow. They walked around the house and Hanna stopped. "Rita, last night there was a large fire in the woods, with flames leaping far above the tree line and I heard screaming most of the night. The wailing and shrieking was deafening. But now, nothing. Not a sign of anything."

Rita stood gazing into the woods. Rita could see no indication of a fire at all. "Where was the fire?" she asked.

Hanna went over to her. "That is just it. The fire consumed the entire forest. It was so freighting. I could see it. I could smell it." she said visibly still shaken. "But today it's as if it didn't happen at all.

Rita's heart was pounding. Could this mean Annie was dead? Rita and Hanna stood there not talking, just looking towards the forest. Then they both turned and walked back to the house. When they were in the house it seemed okay to speak and Rita broke the silence.

"All is not lost. It can't be." she said. "Annie is still alive. If she were dead, I would feel it in my heart." Rita walked back outside and sat down on the steps, looking towards the woods. Hanna turned and went into the kitchen. She knew Rita needed time alone. Rita felt a sadness sweep over her like a dark cloud. She unleashed a flood of tears that shook her whole body.

After what seemed like an entirety she wiped her eyes and slowly got to her feet. Rita walked to the side of the house, stopped and looked towards the woods. Slowly she moved forward, as if being drawn towards something. As she drew nearer, she saw movement. Going closer she realized there was someone or something in the woods. Rita moved closer still and saw several people moving in a slow and almost painful manner. Rita thought she recognized Annie in the distance. She called to her but there was no response. It was like looking at a large movie screen. But there was no distinct outline around it, everything on the edges reminded Rita of the heat waves you would see rising off of hot cement in the heart of summer. All Rita could do was watch. Then she saw a man go up to the woman who looked like Annie, as if to speak to her. She turned and ran after him, barley keeping up. Rita sensed something was very wrong but could not communicate with Annie. Rita rushed to another part of the woods but she could not enter the forbidden "other time." Totally frustrated, she stopped and stood still.

Hanna had been watching out the window, concerned for her young friend. Now she rushed up to Rita. "What is going on?" she asked, but all Rita could do was look at the woods and the people moving away, to where she did not know. The only sounds were that of people weeping and the moaning from the wounded. All there was to see was destruction and smoke.

Rita turned to look at Hanna, "What can we do? There must be something. There must be." Her voice was full of sadness and despair. All Hanna could do was put her arms around Rita.

"I don't know dear. There is no way to reach your friend. We just have to trust her to take care of things the best she can."

Rita looked once more at the woods and turned and went back to the house with Hanna. Rita stayed with Hanna but her heart was too heavy to enjoy the companionship. She decided to go back to town. As Rita was leaving she paused and looked towards the trees one more time.

"Annie can take care of things." she said out loud.

Hanna nodded her head, "Right she can, dear. No reason to worry your pretty head."

Rita drove back to town. Perhaps seeing William might help. She walked into the dealership and spotted him talking to a man who looked very serious. She paused and waited for him to finish when all of a sudden he spotted her and acknowledged her with a nod. The two men talked a minute and shook hands. The man did not look serious any longer as he went towards the door. William came over to Rita.

"Is there a problem?" she asked.

"No," William answered, "he ordered a special edition and there has been a slight delay in the delivery, probably a problem at the factory. He is just being impatient."

"I need a drink." Rita said. "Would you like to join me?"

"Don't mind if I do." William said with a twinkle in his eye. Taking Rita's arm and guiding her outside. As they walked down the cobbled stone street he continued. "You look troubled. Do you want to tell me about something? Maybe I can solve it for you."

Rita stopped and looked at him, "You would think I am completely crazy if I told you my problem."

William took her arm again and they continued on, eventually turning into a little pub. "Let's talk about it over a glass of wine." After a few sips of the Merlot he ordered for Rita, she found herself relaxing. "Now my dear, lets have it."

Rita looked up at William. "Have what?" "Whatever the worried look was all about."

"Oh, it was just frustration. All the dead ends I have run into with the research of my ancestors that I have been doing in my spare time."

"Well that is one thing I can't help you with. All I know is my ancestors came from this general area and then spread out through England over the past couple hundred years. The family kept up with it and I was even named for some great great great grandfather way back in the dark ages." he laughed. William took a drink of his beer smiled. "He was some kind of warrior or something to that effect. I guess one could say he sacked the countryside back in his time. There is a sword that my father had that belonged to some bloody bloke who was a big time land owner back in the fourteenth or fifteenth century. I never could get into that sort of history."

Rita's head cocked to one side "Who was this land owner?" she asked.

"I don't think my father ever knew his name, at least no written proof of the fact, just an old relic sword from the past." William laughed, "I prefer looking ahead not backwards and I see a bright future." Rita felt her face flush. No man had ever looked at her the way William was right now. "Let's have some brunch and then we will go somewhere and do something that will take your mind off your problems and make you smile again."

The rest of the day turned out to be full of excitement and laughter. Too soon it was time to go back to the hotel. As Rita lay starring at the ceiling she went back over the events of earlier that day. What could have happened and where did Annie go as she was running away in a panic. Was Robert or Joey hurt? Why couldn't Rita get to her? Joey had come through the time barrier. What was stopping her? I have to stop thinking about it for now. I have to sleep. There are too many things to finish tomorrow. I must get out of this hotel and into my home. Rita thought about Annie again, got out of bed and went over to the window, pacing nervously. "Annie, what can I do to help?" Rita said out loud to the vast darkness. After what seemed like an eternity Rita went back to bed. She still couldn't sleep.

The dawn came slowly. Not until the sunshine streamed brightly through the windows, did a worn out Rita get out of bed and head for the shower. "I have to think of a way to reach Annie." Rita thought. "But right now I need to finish with the house."

Chapter 22

While Annie worked on Robert's wound, one of his men explained what had happened. James the Terrible raided and burned down most of the village. An undetermined number of villagers had died. If they didn't die in their homes as they burned down, they were killed by the marauders when they ran to avoid the fires. The dead were covered up until they could be given a proper burial. Robert and his men fought both the raiders and the fires the best they could. James and his band of cutthroats finally rode off, passing the manor on the way and inflicting damage there as well. He wasn't sure at what point Robert had been wounded.

"Well, the good news is his wound isn't too bad. The arrow isn't deep. I'll get it out and clean and bandage it. He will be okay soon. Take him up and put him in his bed. Sleep is what he needs now."

Annie paused as a knock sounded at the door. Several women from the village came in to help. They went up to Annie with a hug and an offer to help any way they could. The women went from man to man checking the wounds and cleaning them so Annie could evaluate them.

After Annie cleaned and dressed wounds of Robert and his men, she began to attend to the villagers that were coming to her for help. Looking outside she saw several people sitting or standing patiently, all needing some kind of care. She looked around and said, "We have a lot to do."

Lillie kept food and drink available for everybody. Even Joey, with just one arm totally useful, and the other carefully covered so no one would see the strange cast, did what he could fetching clean bandages and water for Annie as she requested them. Most injuries were superficial and were taken care of without too much trouble. As the day went by,

Annie wondered if the stream of villagers would ever end. But still people need attention and she kept on going.

It was afternoon when Annie stopped at one man to check his wound and saw the slash would not close unless it was stitched. She turned to one woman who had been assisting her. "Go to my sewing room and bring back a very sharp needle and thread."

"Yes Mum." She answered as she turned and left.

Annie began cleaning the man's wound. The woman returned with the needle and thread. "This is going to be very painful," Annie told the man, "and it is going to leave an ugly scar."

"It'll match t' the others." he laughed.

"Please, be still. I will try to be quick about this." she said. The stitches were not like she remembered but they would have to do. The woman that brought the needle and thread was staring at the stitches in utter amazement. Annie asked for some clean bandages and promptly got the wound covered, hoping the stitches would hold.

All the time, while Annie tended to the injured man, one of the village women kept an eye on every move she made. It wasn't out of curiosity or admiration for her work, but much more of a suspicious nature. Sensing something could be wrong; one of Robert's men stepped in between them and pushed the other woman away. But the damage had been done. The woman looked at Annie with fear in her eyes. Realizing she had just done something no one had done before; Annie knew she had to explain her action to the startled woman. With several people still needing attention, now was not the time to start a controversy. Annie turned to the women and tried to explain how she had to sew the cut closed so it would not get infected.

"Who tol' you how to do that!" the old woman shouted, "The devil?"

Everyone in the room stood still and stared. The silence was deafening. A loud voice shattered the stillness as Robert pushed through the crowd. "What do you mean, *devil*? You leave her alone, ol' hag!"

"She is a witch!" she screamed while lifting the makeshift bandage and exposing the haphazardly sewn wound. "Look at what she did to that poor man."

A couple of men dragged the screaming woman away, but Annie could see that others were leaving also, whispering amongst themselves, pointing and looking to see what Annie had done.

"Come lass," Robert said, "you need some rest. You've been at it all day. These fine ladies can finish what's left." He motioned to the only two women who had stayed behind. Sheepishly, they nodded an acknowledgement, and continued to work on the few remaining injured. Annie leaned on Robert as he led her outside. "Go. Sit by the tree. I'll be right back." he directed.

It had been a long and exhausting day. Annie was overwhelmed with all the pain the people had endured. Last night had not been restful and then interrupted by the fire. She had been up half the night, and now she realized the sun had set on another day. It was now late into the evening. Just about everyone was cleaned and all the wounds were dressed. She could see Lilly and another lady back in the house, passing out water and food to the people still there one more time. Annie sat down by the big old tree. She was gazing up at the stars thinking how peaceful they were and started to fall asleep, not realizing how utterly tired she was.

Robert's deep voice opened her eyes again, "Lass, here drink this." He said handing her a cup of wine.

Annie sat up feeling a bit refreshed and slowly got to her feet. "Have I been asleep long? Is everyone okay?" she asked.

"About 30 minutes, yes, Lass, everyone is ok. We lost fifty men that we know of. About thirty were taken away.

Annie looked around. There seemed to be so much destruction. The manor looked as though it were half gone. Angus and a few men were working on the other side of the manor, using torch light, taking down burned and charred cross beams before they fell on their own. Robert had assured her it was not as bad as it looked. "We have moved most of the wounded into the stable, until they are able to get home on their own." Robert said. "And I have made a place in the barn for you and Joey. I don't think you should stay in the house tonight. We have to be sure the upper floor will hold. Angus can check it better tomorrow in the daylight. I think you need some rest now.

Remembering the old woman and her accusations, she said, "There is going to be trouble, isn't there?"

"Yes, lass. I'm afraid there could be trouble. But you need to rest now. We will talk later after a good night's sleep."

Joey was brushing his pony as Robert and Annie went into the stable.

Annie lay on the fresh straw and went fast asleep. Robert told Joey to put things away and to go lay down by Annie. Then he went outside, wondering how much trouble the old woman could stir up and what could happen. He knew all to well when someone was accused of witchcraft, how crazily people reacted. Suddenly it was very clear to him what needed to be done. He saw Angus going around the house and started toward him. When Robert caught up with him, he was telling his helpers to go home for the night and return at first light to continue. After they left, Robert told him to get things ready for a trip. He was to take Annie and Joey to France.

"I will join them in a few weeks after I get things settled here." Angus did not need an explanation. He set about loading a wagon for the trip. He needed to hurry for the ship to France would be leaving within a week.

"How long will we be in France?"

"At least three months. Hopefully the idle gossip will stop by then and then we can all come home. But I want my family safe now. When the next ship leaves, I want everyone on it. Do you understand?"

"It will be done."

Robert went back to the stable and lay down by Annie, praying everything would be okay and that he was doing the right thing.

Chapter 23

It was about mid morning when Rita arrived at the cottage. She walked around admiring the work that had been done. The men had done a wonderful job on the outside with all the stones. Rita was quite pleased with the landscape work as well.

There were rose bushes alone the front of the house and lovely hedges by the road. The painters, having finished outside, were working on the inside since all the carpentry was complete. Today was Thursday and Rita had been told she could move her things in over the weekend. She was very happy to soon be leaving the hotel. The interior decorator called and told Rita that all the furniture had been purchased and was ready to be delivered just as soon as the house was complete. Rita set delivery up for Monday morning.

Rita could not think about the cottage at this moment. She had to get back to the monastery. She wanted to find out everything about the time period that Annie was in. Rita told the man in charge what she expected to be done and to take care of everything because she was leaving for a couple of days. Rita drove to the monastery hoping she would see the monk. Thankfully, he was sitting on the bench out in the yard. The monk stood as Rita approached but Rita waved him to sit back down.

"Hello." Rita said, "I was wondering if there were any records that you have not seen that may have more information about Robert and Annie. If there are, may I see them?"

"My eyes are not good anymore but if you want I can show you where the old records are. Perhaps you can have better luck than I. You can go through them and see if you can find anything at all about Annie and her life."

"Thank you very much. Just show me where they are."

Father Rufus stood up and led Rita into a side entrance to the building closest to them. They walked down a hall to a door marked *Storage*. The monk opened the door, reached in and turned on a light. A single bare bulb glared from overhead and cast strange shadows on the walls. The room smelled stale and was stacked to the ceiling in some places with boxes.

"If there are any records that would be of help to you, they would be somewhere in here. I will leave you alone and check on you later."

"Thank you." She said as the monk walked back down the hall. Well there is no time like the present, Rita said to herself as she started towards the boxes. Rita went through box after box with no results but kept digging. There were copies of census records, land titles, and baptismal records dating back for hundreds of years. She was very careful not to damage anything for some of the documents were very frail. She had lost all track of time when she came across a box with the name "McKenna" on it. She could feel her heart pounding with anticipation as she slowly opened it. She was interrupted as the door opened and the Father Rufus walked in.

"Would you like some tea and biscuits. You have been in here for hours. Surely you must be hungry or at least thirsty."

"Yes, I am thirsty. I didn't realize I have been here that long. But I just found a box I must look into, would you bear with me a minute?"

"Why sure, you go ahead. I'll just be down the hall. The kitchen is the third door to the right. Come when you are ready."

"Thank you, Father." As Rita turned back to the box, the old monk retreated down the hall. Rita looked at the box again. The name on it definitely was "McKenna" and it was dated "1330." She opened it slowly and began to go through it. After a few minutes she realized that the information contained within originally came from a monastery in France and it had nothing to do with Robert or Annie. Disappointed, she closed the box and decided to call it a day. She took a pen from her purse and marked each of the boxes that were already looked at with an "X" in one corner. "Just in case I come back." She said aloud to no one,

"No point in double the work." After looking around the cluttered room once more, she turned out the light, closed the door and walked down the hall towards the kitchen.

Entering the kitchen she was greeted with the aroma of herbal tea and fresh baked biscuits. "Mmm… Smells good in here…" She remarked.

"Thank you," said the monk, "we have become rather adept at preparing food here. Please, help yourself."

As Rita poured her tea and selected a biscuit, she asked "May I come back some other time to look through some more files?"

"Why of course you may." the monk replied. "You are always more then welcome." Rita finished her tea and biscuit. They chatted for a short time before she thanked Father Rufus for his time and hospitality and walked outside.

The night had a chill but was crystal clear. Rita drove back to the hotel and found that William had left several messages for her. When she got to her room she called him. While the phone was ringing, Rita thought about the way he looked at her and held her hand when they were together. She had grown more than fond of him.

Hopefully his feelings were the same. When William answered Rita felt her knees go weak.

"Hello, where have you been all day? I've called several times." He sounded a bit agitated.

"Well, it's nice to be missed." She answered as demurely as possible. "I was at the monastery, looking through old records, hoping to find something about my ancestors. What have you been up to?"

Realizing his tone was less then cordial, he replied, "I'm sorry. I've had a rough day; two salesmen did not come in. Not that it matters, sales are really down. My maintenance department is backed up. I am sorry, just a bit upset I guess. Oh well. Hey! How about I meet you for a drink? Would that be okay? Say in about 30 minutes in the pub around the corner?"

"I can do that. I'll see you there." She said. He okayed it and they hung up. Rita took a quick shower, fluffed her hair, put on some makeup and got dressed in record time. Admiring herself in the mirror, she knew she looked good in a pair of dark beige linen pants and a light sweater. She hoped William would think so too. Rita left the hotel and walked around the corner. The bar was quiet and she sat at the bar with a good view of the front door and waited patiently. When William walked in, she felt her pulse quicken. He was so handsome, his hair was a little rumpled but that only added to his looks. He looked like a model out of a magazine. His eyes lit up when he saw her. He waved and walked over, giving her a warm kiss on the lips.

"What are you drinking?" he asked.

"A scotch and soda would be fine." she answered.

The bartender came over, wiping his hands on the bar towel. "What'll it be, folks?"

"Scotch and soda for the lady and a scotch rocks for me., water on the side. William replied.

Rita was thinking, should she tell him about Annie, they had gotten very close and she did not want any secrets between them. No not yet, maybe another time. I don't want him to think I am a total kook. As they sipped their drinks William asked how the work on the cottage was going.

"Oh, it's going great. I will be moving some things in this weekend. The furniture will be delivered Monday."

"Well we need to plan a party."

Rita looked at this wonderful man and thought to herself. How can I be serious about someone who was so carefree and fun loving? William did not have a worry in the world. Well, except for his business, that is. He had all the money he would ever need. Rita always had to work and struggle for the things she wanted, until Annie left her an inheritance. But still, Rita felt like they came from two different worlds and wondered if they could ever make a life together. William had made hints of getting serious and Rita felt the magnetism pulling her towards him. Still Rita could not tell William what had drawn her to Scotland. Rita was jerked back to reality when William said, "Hey! Are you okay? You seem a million miles away, so much for my company. How is your drink?"

"Oh, I'm sorry, it's good." Rita said taking another sip. "What were you thinking about? I hope it was me."

Rita thought a second; "Actually, I was thinking I might buy a car from you."

"Really, well today may not turn out to be a total bust after all. What kind did you have in mind?

"I think I would like a flashy red sports car." she said.

"Good. We will go and pick one out and with the discount you get I think you will be happy."

Rita glanced up at him, "What discount?"

"Well, let's just say I can give you a deal you can't refuse."

Rita laughed, "I guess it is a good thing to be friends with the owner." William looked at her with a sideways glance and Rita lowered her eyes. "Well maybe more than friends."

"That's more like it." William said smiling. They finished their drinks and went in to the dinning room for dinner. Over dinner they discussed the future. "Do you think you would like to make Scotland your home?"

"I have given that a lot of thought. That is one of the reasons I bought the cottage. I would like to find out if I could practice medicine here. Do you know what I would have to do to get my license? I really have no idea what the laws are or who I should see."

"No, but we can find out. There is a Board of Physicians at the hospital nearby. We can go tomorrow and ask questions."

There was a lot of small talk over dinner. Rita could see the wheels turning in William's mind and wondered what he was thinking. When they were through, Rita asked if they could go to over to see the cars.

"Why I just happen to have a key." William said laughingly. He paid the bill and they walked to the showroom. William punched in the security codes to disarm the alarm and unlocked the door. After he turned on more lights, Rita walked around the showroom, looking at all the cars. One particular car caught her eye.

"Wow! That is the one I want! Only I want it bright red, you know, they call it "candy apple red," with black leather upholstery. And a black rag top."

William laughed, "Why I did not even have a chance to use my sales pressure on you. There is only one thing, that would be a special purchase and I will have to back order it."

"How long will it take?"

"Well, from past experience it should take about four to six weeks."

"That long?" Rita exclaimed.

William laughed again, "However, I believe I can do something about that. I will call tomorrow and they can tell me when it will be coming off of the assembly line. I'll have someone take me to Edinburgh and I'll fly to London and drive it here. That should save several weeks."

"Oh I don't want to cause any problems." Rita said.

William put his arm around her, "Do you think I would let your pretty little car be delivered on a dirty truck? It is very easy to take a few days off and do it myself. Besides I need to go to London about business anyway. It's really not that bad a drive. I should be able to do it in less than a day without any problem, and it will not have to be shoved in with other cars."

"You have 'business anyway'? So I'm not special." She laughed. "Seriously, that would be wonderful. When do you think we could go?

"We?"

"Yes, we! I have nothing else to do now. Everything will be completed at the cottage and I don't want to just sit around with nothing but time on my hands."

"Well if everything goes okay it will probably take a few days."

William walked Rita back to her hotel. "I am anxiously waiting to see your cottage. From your description, it should be very nice. I think it would be a wonderful place to raise a couple of children." William winked at her.

Rita stopped, "What do mean?"

"Well I suspect you will meet a handsome man who will sweep you off your feet and want to settle down and have a family with you."

Rita knew what he was hinting at but did not want to pursue it further. They lingered at Rita's door for a few minutes exchanging small talk. Rita knew William wanted to come inside but she was not in the mood for company tonight. William hid his disappointment well and accepted a kiss instead and said good night.

Rita went inside, sat down for a while with the TV and then went down to the bar to have a cup of tea. There were too many things on her mind for her to sleep right now. She thought more about William. He was very attractive and there was a lot of sex appeal but was that enough to build a marriage on. Rita sipped her tea as thoughts kept running through her head. They have known each other for such a short time, and yet there was chemistry between them that could not be denied. Rita could not think about it until she knew Annie was okay, there had to be a way to find out what happened. Rita finished her tea and went outside. Maybe a long walk would help. There was a chill in the air; winter would be here before long. Rita walked for several blocks and then went back to the hotel only to find a message from William wishing her a good night. With that thought in mind, she went to bed and was asleep in minutes.

Early the next day Rita went out to the cottage and looked it over. The painters were half finished inside. Soon the furniture could be delivered. That would be Monday so she had the weekend to get moved out of the hotel. Rita closed the front door and got into the rental car and headed to Hanna's. Upon arriving, Rita saw Hanna standing at the edge of the forest, staring into it. Rita called to her as she walked past the house.

Hanna turned and Rita saw a strange look oh her face. "What is going on?" Rita asked.

"Sometime around dawn, I heard a commotion out there." Hanna pointed toward the area where they had found Joey. "When I came out, I saw men working on an old house. It looked as if it were possibly damaged by fire. I heard one man say they better do a good job because Master Robert said Lady Ann would be due back in a couple of months."

Rita walked over to the edge of the woods but could not see anything except for trees. She turned to Hanna, "I guess that means Annie is okay and she must have gone somewhere."

"Well there is nothing there now." Hanna replied, turning to Rita, "Nice to see you again. What did you drive all the way out here for? Is anything wrong?"

"No. Not really. I have been worried about Annie and I'm glad that it seems she is okay. The real reason was to invite you to my new house some time next week for dinner. I want you to meet William also." Hanna eagerly accepted. "I will call you when I know for sure what day it will be."

They visited for a brief time, before Rita left. She felt much better now as she drove back to town. So she went to the dealership to see

William. He was very pleased to see Rita smiling and told her so as he bent over and kissed her.

"I called about your car. It will be completed next Monday. We can leave Tuesday to pick it up. We could be back Wednesday or Thursday if you would like to take in some of the sites of London while we are there." he said with a wink.

"I would like to make it a few days, if you can get off." Rita told him. "Then you can show me the town. And I can pick up a couple of pictures I bought when I first got here."

"I can't think of anything I would rather do. Just let me check with the boss. Ha! That would be me! Why of course I can have off." William said.

Rita told him she had invited Hanna to a sort of house warming dinner that she was planning sometime after she gets moved into the cottage.

"Well, I get to meet this friend that I have wondered about."

The weekend was full of excitement. The cottage was finished by Saturday morning and Rita completed all the arrangements to get everything into the cottage as soon as possible and planned for her dinner Monday evening. She spent Sunday moving out of the hotel. She called Hanna and told her when she would be by to pick her up.

Then Monday came. The furniture was delivered and everything was perfect. Rita looked at the clock and told William she had to leave to pick up Hanna and she would cook dinner when she got back. The trip to Hanna's took a little longer than Rita thought and when they pulled up in front of the cottage a catering truck was pulling out. William met them at the door with an apron tied around his waist.

"What is going on here? I was going to cook." She said as she entered the room and saw a small feast laid out.

"How can we visit if you are in the kitchen? Now you can relax and let me serve you two beautiful women."

Hanna leaned over and told Rita, "Honey, you better put a ring on his finger before I do." Rita felt her face flush because she knew William had heard her.

William took Hanna's hand in his, leaned over kissed it lightly. "You must be Hanna. I have heard a lot about you and have looked forward to meeting you."

"Thank you." Hanna giggled.

"Now please take your seats while I serve dinner. The dinner was wonderful and William was the perfect host, he even mixed and served cocktails.

It was midnight when they took Hanna home. It had been a perfect night. Rita told Hanna she was going to be gone for a few days. They talked for a while, and then William and Rita left.

William had gotten the plane tickets and was there bright and early Tuesday morning to pick up Rita. The flight was short and soon they were deplaning. William had booked a rental car and a hotel.

"We can pick up the car this afternoon, if you would like to get some rest now." he said. They had only slept a couple of hours the night before and Rita was very tired. "I booked two rooms but if you want I can change that." William said with a smile.

"I think it would be nice to share a room." Rita said. The suite was large with a hot tub and a balcony that overlooked the city.

They got a little sleep and were soon on their way to see the car. The man gave the keys to Rita and the paperwork to William. She slipped behind the wheel and as she touched everything, she couldn't believe this was really hers.

"Well get in, handsome." she said to William, "and I will take you to dinner." Smiling, he slipped in to the passenger side and waved his hand, "Let's go, madam."

The days passed in a blur. They went to the opera and the ballet trying to squeeze in everything possible. Rita took William to the hotel she had stayed at when she arrived. Mr. Madison was delighted to see her again. She gave him her new address and requested he ship the pictures to her at his earliest convenience. He assured her it would be done. William said they were beautiful and would look great at the cottage.

On Friday morning they woke to dark skies.

"Oh, it is going to rain." Rita said disappointedly, "and I so wanted to drive home with the top down."

They got on the highway as the thunder grew closer and louder. Rita laughed, "I hate storms and driving on the opposite side of the highway, but here goes."

They were about a hundred miles out of town when the storm intensified. There was lightening flashing everywhere. The cracks of thunder seemed to cause the little car to shake. It was nothing like Rita had ever experienced before. William was reading the map and telling her where the curves were. "They are going to get worse and keep a sharp eye out for fallen rocks." He said.

Things were going smoothly and Rita began to relax. She asked William to find some music on the radio. As he lifted his eyes up to look back at the road, they were coming around a curve. There in the middle of the road was an enormous boulder.

"Watch out!" he screamed.

Rita had also seen the large rock. She jammed on the brakes and the little car skidded out of control on the wet pavement. She was attempting to correct the spin as the car slammed into a guardrail, flipped over it, went airborne and crashed with the passenger side against a large tree several yards from the road. Rita's head hit the driver's side glass and the last thing she felt was sharp pain radiate down her left leg, then blackness. The only sound left was that of the heavy downpour as it drummed on the mangled car.

Chapter 24

It was a beautiful day in northern France. Annie sat in the sunlight watching Joey play. How calm things are she thought, it seemed like Scotland was a million miles away. Annie wanted to get back but she knew it was impossible right now. The trip here was quite an experience. Just like her honeymoon voyage, it was anything but pleasant. Two weeks on an ancient schooner (to her anyway) in choppy seas was not fun. Joey was still having nightmares about the night of the fire, although they were getting better. His arm was healing and they were able to keep his cast a secret. She would be taking it off in a couple weeks. He still would not stray far from Annie and would often turn around just to see if Annie was still there. Annie knew he was young enough to get over the problem quickly so she was not too worried.

It had only been a week since Robert arrived and he was already biting at the bit ready to get back to Scotland. He knew that James's men had suffered a lot of casualties and the situation with him would be a lot better with James out of the way. Robert knew his men would rebuild the manor and it would be bigger and better. He knew how close he had come to losing Annie and Joey and it would never happen again, he would see to it. Things would be different and a lot safer from now on. Robert looked over at Annie. She had been so strong and brave through the whole thing. She mended and nursed the men back to health and never complained. He saw Lilly walking down the walkway and knew that without her Annie would have had a harder time, the two women worked well together. The days passed slowly but time was what Annie needed. Robert could see that with each day Annie looked better and stronger. Robert had been giving her riding lessons and it was a slow process teaching Annie because she had a fear of any horse that was not Max.

The days passed into weeks. Soon they would be going home but first Robert had to replace a lot of the things that were lost in the fire. There was no better time or place to do it. Robert had the servants hitch the wagon up and put supplies in it as he went to talk to Annie. Annie saw the men fussing around and knew something was up so she was ready when Robert walked up to her. Annie put her hands on her hips and tapped her foot.

"Just how long will you be gone and where is it to this time?" she asked. Robert hung his head in mock embarrassment. "Just a few weeks, lass. I have to replace the things that were lost in the fire."

Annie smiled and put her arms around his neck. "Please hurry back. And be careful." She kissed him and he held her close. She knew it would be longer than a few weeks but she knew he would be back as soon as he could. Robert went over to Joey and lifted him for a hug and kiss.

"Daddy," Joey said, "I need a bigger pair of boots I am growing taller. See." He exclaimed as he stretched his legs out to the side.

"I will get you a new pair of boots and a surprise too."

"Thank you daddy." Joey said as Robert lowered him back to the ground. Annie stepped over to the wagon and held onto Robert again to give him a kiss goodbye. The two women and Joey waved as Robert rode out of sight. Annie wiped the tears from her cheek and turned to go help with lunch. Things would be a little lonely without Robert but there was a lot to do and Annie wanted to stay busy.

Workers were still busy rebuilding parts of the castle. But it was going smoothly. Annie spent a lot of time going through all the rooms taking mental notes of things that were needed. The place was cold and damp so there had to be some more fireplaces and more tapestry hung on the walls.

Annie was also busy with the landscaping, supervising the planting of hedges and several varieties of plants and flowers. Lilly and some of the other women from her village had taught her which plants and herbs were good for sickness and other ailments.

A month passed and still Robert did not return. Annie was not too concerned because she knew traveling was difficult and Robert did not push his men very hard. He was very considerate and that was one of the reasons they were all so loyal to him.

Annie had everyone working from morning to dusk every day. No one complained as long as there was plenty of food and drink available. Winter was coming and Annie hoped Robert would be back before the cold weather set in. That was not a good time to sail the North Sea. Annie had learned to weave and had made several pieces of clothing for her and Joey, which she was quite proud of. Next she would try crocheting. There were times she missed her old life but they were becoming few and far between. All in all she was very happy; yes this was her place in time.

Chapter 25

Rita regained conscious slowly. She heard voices but could not imagine who they were. Her eyes opened, or tried to. Something wasn't right. She blinked but it did not help. She tried to reach up and touch her face with her left hand but her arm wasn't able to. She opened her eyes again, realizing her left eye wasn't working properly. She had no way to tell it was black and blue and swollen shut. With her right eye she could see a doctor standing by the bed writing in a chart. She tried to speak but no sound came out. The doctor saw she was awake.

"Well hello, Doctor Richards." he said. "You have been in a coma for a week. We have been quite concerned but not as much as your friend Hanna. She has sat by your bed day and night." Rita mouthed the words 'Where's William?' but nothing came out. She tried to speak again and the doctor responded, "Yes I know. We will take the tube out in a few minutes now that you are awake and then you can talk."

Hanna walked in, saw Rita awake and rushed to her, "Oh honey, you are okay. I have been so worried. You will be up and about in no time. It's going to be okay. Oh, thank you God, thank You." she said with tears on her cheeks.

The nurse came in with a tray and the Doctor told Rita he would take the tube out. Rita closed her eyes took a deep breath and out came the tube. "Where is…" Her voice wasn't there. "Where is William?" she tried again, barely above a whisper.

Hanna backed up a step with her hand to her face. The doctor looked a little uncomfortable. "We will talk about William later. You need to rest now."

"No. I want to know now." Rita's voice cracked as she tried to speak. She struggled to sit up only to fall back again as a wave of pain hit her. She looked up at the doctor, her one good eye pleading. She took a deep breath, which hurt her chest and tried again. "Please doctor, where is William?"

The doctor sat down in a chair next to the bed. Hanna turned her back and stepped away, stifling a sob. Rita felt her throat close in pain. "Doctor Richards," he began. Rita put up her hand to stop him.

"Rita, please call me Rita."

"Rita," he began again, "you were both in a very horrible accident. William was pinned in the car. He suffered a broken neck and died instantly. I am so sorry for your loss. You have multiple injuries, a broken right leg and your left color bone is broken also. Your head hit something resulting in a closed head injury and concussion. That resulted in your coma. I think your eyesight will be okay, however your left eye is swollen and black and blue. Vision from that eye will be impaired for some time. There are several stitches just above your left eye. Your nose is also broken. There were several internal injuries but they are healing nicely. We will let you go home in a few days if you continue to improve." The Doctor stood up and held her hand for a moment. "I know you will have some questions. Right now you need to rest. If you need something, just ask the nurse. I will check in on you later."

Hanna stepped up to the side of the bed. She was dabbing at her eyes with a tissue. She took Rita's hand in her own. "What can I do for you? Can I get you anything?"

Rita shook her head "no' and turned it to the side and the tears began.

"There, there, Love. You go ahead and cry. It will help. I will let you have some privacy, you need to be alone." But Rita only grasped her hand tighter, indicating she did not want to be alone. She had not felt such pain since Annie had gone away. "Okay, I will stay with you." Hanna sat with Rita until she stopped crying and fell fast asleep.

The days went by slowly and she seemed to be in pain constantly. The pain medicine caused her to have terrible dreams and she relived the wreck over and over again. Hanna was there day and night fussing over her, going home only to bathe and change clothes.

Rita was able to go home after two weeks. She was healing nicely but unable to get around without the help of a wheelchair. Even though the cottage was complete and just the way Rita wanted it, she still felt unhappy without William to share it. Hanna made sure it was kept clean and had hired a grounds keeper to help out. Rita knew she could not have handled things alone with William on her mind and was grateful for all the help Hanna had given. Rita could not attend the funeral because she was in the hospital at the time. She wanted to go to the gravesite as soon as she could, but kept putting it off because the pain was too great. As time went by, her injuries healed nicely and the bruises faded away but Rita's heart was still broken.

Three months passed and Rita started thinking about going back to the states. There was nothing to keep her here any longer. Rita went to William's grave to say good-bye and while standing there she realized she wanted to stay in Scotland. It was like a new beginning and she needed a new start in life. She laid flowers on William's grave, threw him a kiss and slowly walked away. "I will check into getting my license to practice medicine here." Rita thought to herself. "I will just keep busy doing what I love and things will be just fine. That is what William would have wanted." She got into her car and headed towards her home and Hanna. The sun was shinning for the first time in days and Rita's heart felt a little lighter as she drove into the driveway and saw Hanna standing on the porch waiting for her.

"I'll spend a lot of time working in the yard, doing things that I always loved doing, making things grow." she thought. There wouldn't be time for much else and that is the way she wanted things to be. Everything happens for a reason, she would deal with what life has in store for her and life will go on. Knowing this was where Annie wound up, as crazy as it might seem, there was always a chance to go back in time or for Annie to appear in this time. Normal people would think this to be preposterous but Rita knew better and wanted to stay.

"Yes, I think I will stay." Rita said to herself, "This is my home, now." Rita got out of the car, climbed the porch steps and went into the cottage with Hanna.

THE END

Or is it just the beginning…?

CPSIA information can be obtained
at www.ICGtesting.com
Printed in the USA
LVHW032304101022
730380LV00003B/87